Racing the Wind

Racing the Wind

Spending our Youth in Small-Town America

Continuing the Award-Winning Dancing Deer Series with Book Eight

Ron Lambert

Copyright © 2015 by Ron Lambert

Published in the United States by:

Printers Guild Publishing House

425 Spring Street, Suite 101
Columbus, Texas 78934-2461
(979) 732-2963
Fax (979) 733-0015
www.printersguildpublishing.com

ISBN 978-0-9855083-8-8

Trademarks

Racing the Wind is a work of Fiction

Except for some historical personages, the names, characters, and incidents of the story are used fictitiously and do not represent any actual person or event.

Some of the towns, cities, or geographic localities are real. An interested reader might find Lee Mountain, the Buffalo River, the Illinois Bayou, the Big Piney, Moccasin Gap, or even Little Creek's water crossing. Eudy's Drug and Fountain might be harder.

The author grew up in a small, rural community and saw wonder in all living things. He wrote this story using the hazy remembrances of a child's fertile imagination and sheer luck.

Cover

Photo by Fenner Photography

Contents

CHAPTER 1 – BILL PROPOSES A RACE
May, 1946

Bill reached for the paper. It was time to take a breather. He had always wanted to see the world, but after a few trips to foreign ports, it was time to stay home for a while. Harriet had moved back after being away for eighteen years, and he didn't want her to become bored and leave again. So Bill had taken Harriet on a belated honeymoon to Yellowstone National Park. They spent leisure afternoons watching geysers spit sulfur laden water, bears catch flying fish, and buffalo run wild. With a new pair of binoculars, he enjoyed a great time until he decided to try his hand at wilderness hiking. Getting too close to a bear cub, Bill broke his leg while sliding down a rock escarpment. The cub's distraught mother had only chased Bill a short distance before his slide. She looked down the sheet of loose shale at a crumpled intruder then returned to her baby probably thinking the intruder was more of a threat to himself than to junior.

Bill worried that he would appear weak if his business associates pictured him running away from anything, so he sent a postcard home saying he broke his leg learning to ski. Bill spent the remainder of his stay in the resort bar, with his leg in a cast, drinking the establishment out of liquor, and pondering what would have happened if he had not slid his way out of a difficult situation.

Back in Dancing Deer, Bill hobbled around on crutches. He used up his accumulated goodwill having things brought to him, or his other needs attended to—like turning on the radio. He tried to resupply the lost goodwill by taking Harriet to South America once the cast was removed. They ate mountains of beef in Argentina, drove the scariest road in the world in Peru, and danced holes in their shoes in Brazil. But right now he needed a rest. He'd stay home for a while, take care of his bank, and provide the town with a few more anonymous gifts.

Bill wasn't sure if he liked being the anonymous benefactor because of how much his projects improved the town or the fun he had watching the nervous twitch of the town populace as they wondered who was buying them out and for what purpose. Everyone was a little uneasy when a new project made the paper. Trees had been planted, sidewalks expanded, public bathrooms installed, a city park constructed around Mr. Ridley's thermal spring, and the clock on the courthouse repaired. He'd even sent an organ to a church in Springfield, Missouri.

Holding a cup of coffee by thumb and index finger of one hand and clutching a copy of Dancing Deer's semi-weekly newspaper with the other, Bill went looking for a comfortable chair. A chair not covered with unpacked suitcases, sacks of painted gourds, bead necklaces, or a humongous shark mouth populated with multiple rows of triangular, serrated teeth.

"Honey, what are you going to do with all these . . . these souvenirs?"

"Bill, those are yours. I bought clothes for me. Maybe you should consider opening a museum. Think in terms of tourist draw."

"Naw. I'll use them to decorate my office. I'm thinking in terms of office draw."

"Bill, do you know anything about that new race they're building a track for in Skunk Hollow? Your concierge told me to ask if you were aware of what they're doing down the road."

"No."

"He told me to make sure you read that paper you have."

Ten minutes later Bill was on the telephone to Jesse Bell, the owner and editor of the *Marsden County Meteor*. From Jesse's paper, he had learned a new person was in charge of the bank in Skunk Hollow and had set a plan in motion to gather credibility, community awareness, and positive public perception. To no one in particular Bill said, "I've shot them down before, and I can do it again."

"Shot who down?"

"Jesse, I'm sorry; I was thinking out loud. But what I need to know is how we can get Skunk Hollow's application put on hold while the Dancing Deer City Council prepares one for us. Dancing Deer needs to have that race not those hooligans in Skunk Hollow."

"I think you're too late, Mr. Potter. Officials from Akron have already scheduled an assessment trip. If they find Skunk Hollow their best candidate then next summer, the All-American Soap Box Derby Association is going to have a local race in Skunk Hollow."

"And what does that mean?"

"Next summer derby officials will come to Skunk Hollow and set up shop to administer the races. Skunk Hollow will have built a racetrack according to contest rules, the entrants will have their racers weighed and inspected, and there are numerous other formalities adhered to—and checked. They have a rulebook you wouldn't believe. I think, Mr. Potter, while you were having a good time traveling, a new banker in Skunk Hollow has scooped you. I say that seriously because, as a newspaper editor, there is nothing worse than being scooped by your competition."

"If they're coming down here why can't they give us a look see? What are they coming down to assess? Wait a minute. Skunk Hollow has two rundown hotels and a few greasy spoons. How many people will this race bring to town?"

"A thousand or more. I've looked up a few stories through the Associated Press, and each local race has a hundred or more boys bringing their racers. So if the average family has four people and a hundred families bring a boy and a racer there's four hundred right there. Then there are their friends, extended relatives, well-wishers, general racing fanatics, and the officials putting on the race with their families. A thousand seems plausible to me."

"And where will those people stay? Where will they eat? Where will they shop?"

"In Skunk Hollow. The new banker has connections. He's bringing new businesses into town. Their newspaper says they'll have a larger and more dynamic business scene than Dancing Deer in five years. Land prices have already skyrocketed as developers are buying every inch available. I've heard that the mayor is the one responsible for talking his college roommate, a very charismatic fellow, into moving here from Phoenix. This new guy has gotten local backing involved with scads of money and has brought with him a storm of ideas he wants to put into play. And the bank was where he started."

"They have a newspaper?"

"Yep. The *Skunk Hollow Fever* publishes every Friday. They've taken some of my advertisers, and my circulation has decreased slightly.

"Jesse, you can't let them do this to your business. Your dad worked too hard to let you get it buried by an upstart. If you need money to modernize or to expand, I've got it for you."

"Thanks, but after buying that new offset press a few years ago, I garnered all the debt I can handle. Besides, the other town in our part of the country the officials are looking at is Little Rock. And in Little Rock they have plenty of rooms and upscale restaurants. Skunk Hollow can't compete with Little Rock."

CHAPTER 2 – HOWDY LEARNS THE BITTER TRUTH

December, 1926

Howdy Monroe caught a ride with his best friend, Asa Thompkins, to spend Christmas break in Skunk Hollow. Both boys attended college at the University of Texas in Austin and needed a rest from the rigors of a stressful collegiate curriculum. Asa had promised Howdy they would have a quiet time in a pretty, rural setting. Sleeping would be their main intended activity. There was only one party scheduled—a welcome home soiree given by Asa's parents and younger sister, Sydney Rene. After that they would be catered to by servants, allowed to sleep till noon, be fed on the terrace or in the garden, and participate in an occasional card game until it was time for an afternoon nap. Howdy had been looking forward to the daily grind of college life being only a hazy remembrance.

Howdy and Asa had their last class Thursday afternoon and left in Asa's two-seat sports car immediately after its completion.

"Old chap, don't pay any heed to my dad or grandpa. They are men of business, and if you can't contribute any interesting trivia or news from the business world, they won't have anything to do with you. They'll think you're not worth the space you're taking up. My mom goes around telling the servants what to do and apologizing to everyone else for her husband and his father."

"Didn't you tell me the members of your family were bankers?"

"Yep, that's the whole problem. Grandpa inherited the Peoples Bank and Trust of Skunk Hollow from his dad. It came with limited resources, a small group of solid supporters, and a determined adversary trying to bury the bank under his heels."

"So, Asa, you're majoring in finance so you can take over the business and put the skids on this determined adversary?"

"Pretty much. I wanted to be a historian and teach at the collegiate level, but that was not in line with the agenda of the ones holding the money. I was told my future was in banking or if I decided otherwise, riding the rails with a small sack of clothes hanging on a stick."

Howdy said, "And, because your interests lie on different streets, you squeak by with barely passing grades. I'm glad my parents are more reasonable. Dad told me I could be anything I wanted, but I had better be the best there was at whatever I chose."

"But you're majoring in accounting. That's such a boring field."

"Not for me, Asa. I like putting things in order. Give me a pile of papers, a shoebox of ledger tickets, a sack of receipts, or a warehouse of inventory and set back to watch me organize, sort, separate the inconsequential, discard the garbage, and assimilate whatever remains into some cohesive, logical arrangement."

"Howdy, we must've gotten mixed up at birth. Do you think it's too late to change places? You would be much better at duking it out with Bill Potter. I just want to read about famous people, ancient civilizations, and what drove us to what and where we are right now."

"Is this Bill Potter your dad's enemy?"

"Yeah. And his father and his grandfather before that. The Potters and the Thompkins have been bitter enemies since . . . since forever."

"How'd it start?"

"No one knows. He'll do something to make our life miserable, and we have to retaliate. And when we do he has to do something reciprocal. It's just a round robin of nasty tricks played on us by the Potters and by us on them."

"Why don't the two families get together for a pow-wow? One of you could say, 'We'll quit if you will.'"

"Naw, that wouldn't work. Potter would want to quit when he was ahead and my dad would want the same advantage. Acquiescing when you're the aggrieved party tells everyone you're weak."

"And no one wants to be thought of as being weak. It's not manly." Howdy leaned back in his seat thinking how he could use this bit of information for his benefit. Before long his head slid to the crack between the door and his car seat, cushioned only by his hand. He didn't wake until they reached Texarkana.

When Asa stopped to refuel, Howdy shook his head to get rid of the cobwebs and asked if Asa needed relieved from driving for a while.

"Naw, I got it. I've been looking forward to this for three months. I've got a girl back home who I can't wait to see."

"Why haven't you said anything? Is there any other secrets you're harboring under a cloud of hidden agendas?"

"Just that none of my family knows about her. And I want to keep it that way."

"Great scott, man. We're in the twentieth century. Marriages aren't arranged anymore. You can date or marry anyone you please."

"And, Howdy, you don't live in the real world. Everything I have, everything I want, everything possible is controlled by the people with the money—and that is not me. If I were to do something against my family's wishes I'd find my car taken, my college tuition in arrears, and my clothes missing. Even the servants would ignore me. My life as I now know it would be taken until I woke up, faced reality, and got back in line."

"And that would be . . .?"

"That would be majoring in finance, marrying Beatrice Baxter, and taking over management of the bank."

"That doesn't sound all that bad—wait a minute, what does this Baxter woman look like?"

"She's tall, a little overweight, and loud."

"And these are characteristics that pervade the entire clan and are mannerisms you can't tolerate?"

"And the fact that Beatrice is not Isabelle."

"Asa, you have a problem."

As the sun was setting, long shadows extended over the two-lane road. Asa turned from the highway and descended into a verdant valley by way of a winding paved path without center stripes or signs.

"Asa, how much farther?"

"Just a bit. We are now on our land."

Well, I have to admit this is beautiful. In Phoenix, our landscapes are all some variety of desert. We don't have enough water for this. Is that a lake I see in the distance?"

"Yeah, the house backs up to it."

"Where is Skunk Hollow? Does your family own that too?"

"No. If we had followed the main road another mile or so, we would have entered town. It's not big and doesn't have as many businesses as Dancing Deer, but we manage. There are four affluent families, a few in dire circumstances, with everyone else considered middle class."

So the Thompkins are one of the affluent four and Isabelle, a member of one in dire circumstances?"

"No, her family has a little money. She's just not a Baxter."

"So what makes the Baxters so important?"

"They own the lake and a huge parcel of land on the far side."

"I see. Your family wants you to marry a Baxter so the land and the lake can be administered by a Thompkins."

"As well as the bank. The Baxters are the largest minority stockholder."

"Okay, Asa, good buddy. Here's what I'm going to do for you. While I'm here for the holidays, I'll run interference. Anytime Beatrice comes near, I'll step in and charm her to the point you are not even a passing interest. You'll have plenty of time to re-acquaint yourself with Isabelle. Now is that not a good Christmas present or what?"

"The best. But I know you better than you think I do, and I know that you don't go out of your way for anyone unless you get something in return. So, what is it you want from me?"

"I'll let you know."

CHAPTER 3 – HOWDY MAKES AN IMPRESSION

December, 1926

When Howdy and Asa arrived, Asa's entire family poured out of the mansion to deliver a hardy welcome. The servants carried in the luggage and held the door open. A man, by the name of Wilkins, offered to park Asa's sports car.

Asa introduced Howdy as his best friend and roommate. Asa's father wanted to know what kind of work Howdy's father did, Asa's grandfather wanted to know what field of study Howdy had chosen, Asa's mother wanted to know if Howdy was betrothed, and Sydney Rene, Asa's younger sister, wanted to know how old he was and what part of the country he called home.

Asa said, "All in due time. Let's not overwhelm Howdy with our interests into his inner-most secrets. I think he and I both would like to sit in a comfortable chair, have something refreshing to drink, and let you tell us what's going on in the Skunk Hollow community." To Howdy, Asa turned and said, "Come on, buddy I'll show you where you can freshen up."

As the group went into the house Howdy lowered his head and whispered to Asa's younger sister, "Twenty-two. And for your second question: America's southwestern desert—a small town called Phoenix."

Asa walked Howdy to one of the guest bedrooms on the second floor. "We have several available guest rooms but this is the only one with a bath. Any other guests will have to share the one off the hall. Barnes has probably already put your stuff away." As he said this a heavyset woman came through the bedroom door and curtsied.

"Mr. Monroe, your room is ready."

Asa replied for Howdy, "Thank you, Barnes." Asa then turned to Howdy, "Remember, a coat and tie are required for the evening meal. But you have plenty of time to change. Right now anything casual will work. Please be careful not to mention or ask about Isabelle. Please."

"Asa, you don't have to worry about me. I can keep a secret."

"Just as long as you know the terrible consequences that would follow a slip of the tongue."

"I'll be careful." Howdy slapped Asa on the back and went into his bedroom. It wasn't just a bedroom. It was a large suite with a separate dressing room, a private bath and changing area, and a glass wall containing a double glass door opening onto a terrace. His room didn't look out over the gardens behind the house or the lake past the gardens; that view must be reserved for the family. No, Howdy's room looked over the circular driveway and the manicured lawn and fountain in front of the house.

Howdy wondered how many servants there were, what the rest of the house looked like, what kind of car Asa's father drove, how old Sydney Rene was, and if these Baxters lived in similar circumstances. Could he marry for wealth? While he leaned against the railing on the terrace and pondered these issues, a long, black car drove up. Wilkins opened a passenger door, and two young girls in their late teens got out and ran to the house.

Howdy had only packed one jacket, so he searched through his clothes and pulled out a soft turtleneck sweater to wear over corduroy slacks. When he emerged from the bedroom, he could hear spirited conversation downstairs, so he descended to join the party.

"Sydney, I love the way your house is decorated. And I can smell gingerbread. Have Asa and his friend arrived?"

"Yes. Asa is in the drawing room with Dad. And Asa's college friend will be down in a minute. Remember not a word to anyone. Our surprise has to remain intact."

Howdy stood at the bottom of the stairs. "I love surprises. What am I supposed to keep secret."

The two girls started giggling, while Sydney turned red in the face. "This is Mr. Howdy Monroe. Mr. Monroe, let me introduce you to Lucy Lamar." Sydney pointed to a blond who timidly held up a hand and wriggled four fingers.

"And this is Patricia Kilburn. We call her Trish." Trish smiled and held out her hand to Howdy.

"Pleased to meet you ladies. Now, please tell me what I have to keep just between the four of us."

Sydney said, "Since you don't know we'll have to keep it that way."

"Does Asa know what it is?"

"No and it would be a miscarriage of justice to inform him there is anything a foot."

"Hmm, you read Sir Arthur Conan Doyle, do you?"

"On occasion."

Asa walked into the room and found Sydney and Howdy staring at each other. "Oh, here you are Howdy. I see you've met Little Miss Perfect and her coterie. Ladies, if you will excuse us I have to present Howdy to the powers that be." With that said Asa walked over to Howdy and said, "Come on, old chap, we have to get this out of the way."

When Howdy and Asa entered the drawing room three men were seated in a semi-circle around a low table strewn with papers. They stood to shake Howdy's hand while Wilkins placed another armchair next to the one Asa had just plopped into.

Asa introduced Howdy first to Dane Baxter, the neighbor across the lake, and then to his grandfather and father.

The older of the three men said, "Asa says your father is retired."

"Yes, sir. We had a brick manufacturing plant in Cleveland. He sold it when the city started using concrete instead of bricks for its streets. Of course, there was still the housing market but he thought new products would soon be introduced and he had a ready buyer, so he sold, and we headed west to a dryer climate."

"Did those new products ever make it on the scene?"

"Asphalt is now the product of choice for streets. In the housing and commercial building industries, brick and glass on a steel frame are used mostly for upper scale buildings with stucco, tile, and wood taking over for smaller structures or for when pricing is the main concern. Dad's glad he sold when he did. He now plays golf three times a week and takes my mom to Europe twice each year."

Mr. Baxter said, "Well, timing is everything. Burris says you're getting a degree in bookkeeping."

"Burris?"

Asa's father weakly raised his hand. "That would be me. Asa mentioned it in one of his letters."

Howdy continued with, "My degree is in accounting. Bookkeeping is the routine classifying, posting, and summarizing of financial data and displaying it in various financial statements. Public accountants, on the other hand, are the watchdogs who make businesses stick to a uniform way of informing potential investors and creditors how the company is prospering. And accountants in the private sector supply management with the information they need to run their enterprise. Of course, there are lots of other areas of expertise in the accounting field: taxation, international transactions, stock and bond issues, and a host of others. I find it fascinating. Asa is in some of my classes. I think banking and accounting are brothers in the business world."

"Well said, Mr. Monroe. Have you any prospects after you graduate?" asked Asa's grandfather.

"I have an offer to do an internship at The Bank of England. My dad says I ought to spend a year there putting stars on my resume."

"My, my. That is impressive, Howdy. May I call you Howdy, Mr. Monroe?"

"Please."

Hamilton continued with, "Well, Howdy. Is there any one accounting area you are specializing in?"

"Not yet. I still have another year to go for my bachelor's degree, and then I thought I'd spend a year in London before coming back for graduate school."

Burris said, "Quite impressive, Howdy. How are you keeping the women at bay while you plow through your studies?"

"It hasn't been a problem so far. I guess I'm too focused to let extra-curricular activities get out of hand. And my dad keeps telling me how important good grades are."

Dane Baxter turned to Asa. "What about the Texas Longhorn football team? Will they be able to defeat your most hated rival?"

"Texas always has a good football team, but then again, so does our main competition. I guess Oklahoma and Nebraska are our two most hated rivals. Wait a minute. Texas A & M is by far our most hated rival. And, of course, Texas Tech fits in there somewhere. It seems like everyone is gunning for us, and our most hated rival is the one we're playing next.

"When we play the Aggies in College Station, their entire stadium is filled with couples. Every time they score, the male members of the Aggie fan base are required to kiss their dates or, if the fan has just stepped to the concession stand, any woman found unattended. A few years back we went through a period when their team was better than ours and the women at College Station caught up on a term of going without with a term of abundant smacking."

A servant entered the room and announced dinner would be served in fifteen minutes. With this information, Asa and Howdy excused themselves and went to change clothes. Asa's father and grandfather were already dressed for the evening meal, so they remained seated, but Dane Baxter said he had better leave, or he'd miss his evening meal.

CHAPTER 4 – DINNER IN COURSES

December, 1926

Dinner at the Thompkins was a somber occasion. Each participant had a specified seat. Howdy thought Asa's mother must make the assignments after determining who would be attending. Asa's sister and her two friends were at the far end of the table while Howdy sat next to Hamilton, the grandfather.

Everyone sat stock still as the servants brought out the first course. Howdy unfurled his napkin while glancing around the table. They must be waiting for something. The first course was a caesar salad. The old man sitting next to Howdy lifted his fork, speared some lettuce dripping in a creamy yellow dressing and proceeded to put it into his mouth. After the old man had nodded to the servants, the other people around the table began eating.

Howdy thought how the Thompkins' culinary customs differed from what he was accustomed to.

"So, Howdy, why did you pick accounting for your field of study?"

"I've always been a neat person. Everything in its place. No one ever had to clean my room. My dad commented that I would make a good accountant because that's what they do—sort through data and store the numerical representation in various folders. Pretty much like a housekeeper sorts the laundry and puts every item in its place. Socks in one drawer, underwear in another. After a little thought, I decided he was right, and I've been happy with my choice ever since."

"So, being called a 'bean counter' does not offend you?"

"No, that just tells me the person making the characterization is superficial. An accountant is, usually, a detail oriented person sometimes lacking in social skills. We say what we mean in a few well chosen words. There is no excess baggage in our manner of speech. We are not known to be insincere or ambiguous. We get right to the point, rationalize through deductive reasoning, and labor when trying to flatter or say things we don't actually believe. Usually, accountants don't make good dinner guests. But, we don't always fit the stereotype. I, for one, am quite comfortable in social settings." It was time for the soup.

Asa's mother said, "Howdy, you sound like an intellectual. I think you should consider being a writer—not novels necessarily, but how-to books. How to reconcile a bank statement would be a good example. I tried to do that once but couldn't get it done."

"That might be interesting. Maybe, a monthly letter. Anyone subscribing would receive instructions on how to depreciate a capital asset one month and how to declare a dividend in another."

From the other end of the table, Sydney Rene said. "I would find that to be boring. I'd much rather find some capable individual and pay him to handle those tasks."

Asa said, "Has anyone heard the latest on what the AFL is up to?"

"This is getting completely out of hand. What we really want to know is: what are the new fashions in women's clothing? How to make a soufflé? And, what shade of lipstick Carol Lombard wears? Things like that." Sydney stopped talking as everyone at the table was looking her way. "Well, it's what I want to know."

Asa's father said, "Sydney, who will be coming to tomorrow night's party? Did you invite the Baxter girl? Is she coming?"

"I did. She is. And the rest of the guests are mainly Asa's friends from high school." After a short pause, Sydney continued with, "Mr. Monroe, is that how an accountant would answer?"

"I beg your pardon?"

"Mr. Monroe, was that succinct enough? Did you find it flattering or ambiguous?"

"No, ma'am. I found it to be straight to the point and with the right amount of information."

Sydney continued with, "Mr. Monroe, are there many females in your accounting classes?"

"Uh, no. Accounting is a male dominated field of study . . . as is Asa's Department of Finance."

"And why is that, Mr. Monroe?"

"Umm . . . I'm sure, I don't know."

"Could it be that women are not smart enough to delve into the intricacies of a field of study invented by a man who lived in a society where women couldn't work, attend school, or even show their uncovered faces in public?"

"Sydney, I do believe you are smarter than you look. Not many people know that an Arab invented double-entry bookkeeping—not even students learning its ins and outs."

"So now you're saying, I make the appearance of a simpleton."

"No, I am not. I'm saying that a woman, as beautiful as you, has to spend a lot of time achieving that status and couldn't possibly have found enough time to locate such a trivial fact."

"Mr. Monroe, I do not spend all my time primping in front of a mirror. I have more important things to do with my time than to bathe my looks in the shades of glamour men find attractive."

"Sydney, have I done or said something to offend you? I only intended to give you my most profound admiration for your knowledge of something only the most astute of my fellow students would know. And it was truly astonishing that this bit of hidden knowledge came from a woman so young and so pretty."

"Let me think about that. I don't know if you've weaseled out of the hole you'd dug for yourself or if you're escalating the repartee to name calling. And I do not want to be thought of as young."

"I can assure you that I had no intention of demeaning any members of the fairer sex, and especially one with the skills to completely mesmerize me with her charm."

"And this comes from someone who does not flatter and finds it a difficult labor to say something he does not believe in."

"Quite so."

Asa's dad said, "If I might step in here for a minute. Sydney, are you suggesting that you would like to pursue a degree in accounting?"

"I'm not sure, but I don't want somebody telling me I can't because I'm a woman."

Asa's grandfather slid his chair away from the table and suggested everyone retire to the patio where the party could hear the night sounds start as the sun abandons his post.

Howdy was glad to be off the hook for a few minutes. Sydney Rene evidently was a woman who had no problem speaking her mind—especially when there was a wrong needing its head wrung.

In the garden, Wilkins produced a wooden box filled with the pleasant aroma of hand-rolled cigars. He stood before Hamilton Thompkins, Asa's grandfather. Evidently the box contained an assortment of cigars, because, it took the old man several moments to pick one to his liking, Wilkins snipped off the end and used three sulfur-headed matches to light the English market selection corona. Wilkins then handed Asa's grandfather the lit cigar and turned to Burris Thompkins, Asa's father, where the scene was enacted a second time.

Wilkins stood in a striking, posture-perfect pose as Asa cleared his throat. Asa expected to be offered a cigar. Instead, Wilkins took a few steps in Sydney Rene's direction and offered her one. She politely refused causing Hamilton and Burris to murmur something between themselves, Asa's mother to let out a lung full of air, and two of Sydney's friends to blink after staring in disbelief.

Barnes served brandy. Sydney thought she had earned the right to drink with the men, but Barnes was not as amiable as Wilkins and passed her up. Barnes set the bottle down on a small table between the two men and produced a long stemmed glass of white wine for Mrs. Thompkins. Sydney had had her debut as a strong player in a man's field, but she was still a long way from being thought of as the heir apparent.

CHAPTER 5 – BEATRICE

December, 1926

Howdy slept in until nine a.m. That's when Asa knocked on Howdy's door and suggested they go down for breakfast. Howdy asked for thirty minutes and sprinted from the bed to the bathroom. He looked around for his shaving kit before spying it sitting on a window ledge above the toilet.

In thirty minutes, he was knocking on Asa's door.

"Go on down and get yourself some coffee. I went back to bed. I'll be down in thirty minutes. Enjoy a fine breakfast and tell Barnes to bring me a cup of coffee."

Howdy descended the stairs but hadn't made it to the kitchen before Trish, one of Sydney's friends, walked up holding two cups of coffee. "Do you drink it black?"

"I add three teaspoons of cream."

"Come into the kitchen. I have some questions for you to answer while I add the cream."

"What kind of questions, Miss Kilburn?"

"Howdy, I'm not going to bite."

"After doing battle with Sydney, I would be relieved if all you wanted were a chunk of flesh."

"Really? I'm not nearly as argumentative as Sydney Rene. Sometimes a woman can get what she wants without resorting to wrestling it away. The trick is to make the possessor want to give it to you. Some women have that ability."

"Are you one of those women?"

Trish put Howdy's doctored coffee in front of him and sat down before answering. "No. I do not manipulate people; instead I try to earn what I need. I do not borrow things, I do not lend things, and I do not pretend to have what I lack."

"Patricia, you are indeed, an honorable woman. I also live by those same rules."

"So, does that mean I would do well as an accountant?"

"It might. What does your father do?"

"What difference does that make?"

"Only that working for yourself might be more to your liking but carrying on the family business might be more rewarding."

"I see. Well, my father takes pictures. You may have heard of him—Makepeace Kilburn. He's famous in some circles. Travels around the country for *National Geographic*. Right now he's on assignment in South America."

"I guess, Patricia, the only reason your father would need an accountant would be if he retired and opened a studio where he framed and sold his pictures. Have you thought about partnering with him to take the pictures? A man sees things in a masculine way while a woman sees emotion. Plus a woman would put more effort into framing the scene. A man might snap a bullfight with the action of the bullfighter thrusting his sword deep inside the bull's heart; in contrast, a woman might shoot her picture of the bull snorting and pawing at the ground, of the bull gasping for air, or of the matador letting a tear slide down his cheek as he does what he must but with little pride in killing a worthy adversary."

Howdy and Trish looked toward the door as Sydney Rene and Lucy entered. Sydney said, "Trish, I thought you were bringing me a cup of coffee."

"I was, but I got side-tracked by the first of our sleepy men."

"Asa stood at the bottom of the stairs. "Howdy, where's my coffee?"

"Oh sorry, Asa. I was side-tracking."

"You were what?"

"Asa, here work on this while I round up one without cream for you." Howdy handed Asa his cup of coffee.

"Better make that two without cream. I saw Beatrice Baxter ride up on her black stallion as I was leaving my room."

Sydney said, "Beatrice and that horse have similar personalities. He tried to bite me once."

Howdy said, "Does that mean Miss Baxter should be given a wide berth because she bites?"

From the door leading to the garden came, "I do not bite. I might slap, I might kick, I might pull hair . . . gads, I would bite. Stand aside girls, I need a wide berth to approach these two handsome men."

A tall woman in black leather pants stuffed inside black riding boots and billowing out above the knees marched past Howdy and grabbed Asa by his shirt. He winced as Beatrice pulled him close enough to plant a kiss on his mouth. Asa thought about expressing his objection to having two fists of shirt and chest hair yanked free, but said, "Whoa, woman. I'm glad to see you too. Let me introduce you to my best friend, Howdy Monroe."

Beatrice relaxed her grip, patted smooth Asa's shirt, winked at Asa, and turned to the man she had bypassed to get to the man she hoped to marry soon. She held out her hand to Howdy. "Mr. Monroe, if you are Asa's best friend, you must be a special person. My name is Beatrice Baxter."

Holding Beatrice's hand Howdy said, "Miss Baxter, you look stunning. Was it a long ride on your stallion?"

"No, Howdy. May I call you Howdy? I only live on the other side of Baxter Lake."

"Beatrice, I thought our fathers agreed to rename the lake."

"Well, nobody asked me."

Howdy, still holding Miss Baxter's hand, said, "You know, Beatrice, someday you may be giving up the Baxter name in favor of another. If you're the one naming the lake, I think it ought to be 'Lake of the Beatrice.' That way, being named Beatrice would be like having a title—Princess Beatrice. You are a princess aren't you. I recognized it the moment you walked into the room."

"Howdy, I don't know what to say. You've taken my breath away."

"Then I suggest we go outside so you can introduce me to that magnificent Pegasus that flew you over the lake."

"He didn't fly me over the lake. He trotted around the north end."

"Now don't be shy. He could have flown you over the lake. If you trotted around the north end, it must be because you asked him to."

"Asa, I do believe your friend has a gift for flattering women."

Sydney Rene said, "I'll not believe another thing you say, Mr. Monroe. Sir, you talk with a forked tongue."

"Pardon me, Sydney. Did this man tell you he thought you were a princess also?"

"No, he told me flattering someone or saying something he did not believe was difficult for him. That he used few words to express himself and none of it superfluous or ambiguous. What he said he meant. So, Mr. Monroe truly believes you are a princess. Its either that or what he said earlier is a lie, and that was before he had ever set eyes on you."

Sydney turned a half circle and stomped toward the door leading to the garden. She stopped only long enough to say, "Howdy, maybe you can get that stallion to fly you and the princess back over the lake of the Beatrice." She then went through the door slamming it hard on her exit.

"Asa, Sydney's invitation asked me to RSVP, so I came over straight away to welcome you home and to tell Sydney that I will be here for the party. Do you think we could talk somewhere . . . somewhere private?"

"Sure. Let me get us some coffee, and we'll go into the garden." Asa gave Howdy a worried look and his coffee with cream before walking to the countertop where the coffee caldron sat.

Howdy said, "Beatrice, did you go to school with Asa?"

"No. I attended a private school for women in Little Rock. How did you get such a funny name? Is it short for anything? Is your real name Howard or Horace?"

"No, that's my real name. My dad has a sense of humor that knows no bounds."

Asa came back carrying two cups of coffee and suggested he and Beatrice go into the garden as the day was an Indian Summer sort of day with a temperature in the low seventies.

A gardener was planting bulbs nearby and relocated his efforts when he realized he probably should not be privy to the conversation about to take place.

Asa took a sip of the coffee and wiped the sleep from his eyes. "I've just now gotten up. We had a long drive and then had to stay awake late into the night telling my family what a good time I'm having at college."

"Are you having a good time . . . away from me?"

"Now, Beatrice, we've talked about this before. I know we're supposed to marry. It's what both families want, and I'm reconciled to the fact. I'm just not ready."

"Well, you better hurry up. I'm a time bomb. I can't wait forever."

"Is there someone else you're interested in?"

"Of course not, silly. I don't have the patience you do; that's all I'm saying. That and I'm going to France. I won't be back until after you graduate. Will you miss me?"

"Sure I'll miss you."

"And we can get married when I return?"

"We'll see. Okay, Beatrice. I need to go back inside. I haven't had breakfast, and I have a guest to entertain."

"Mr. Asa Thompkins, I'll need one decent kiss and I'll be on my way."

"And a peck and a hug won't do?"

"Absolutely not. And I want to tell you that I know you don't love me. After all, it's an arranged marriage not initiated by either of us. But, for me, I couldn't be happier. I have come to love you these past few years and pray that you'll feel the same about me in time. Asa, I just want to make you happy."

When Beatrice walked back to her stallion, Howdy was waiting. He held the reins to an older and more docile animal. "Could I ride back with you? I'd like to get a close-up view of this beautiful countryside and the Lake of The Beatrice."

Howdy ended up having lunch with the Baxters. From Dane Baxter, Howdy quickly realized that the Baxters owned considerably more land than the Thompkins. But where the Thompkins flaunted their money the Baxters downplayed theirs. The Baxters only had one inside servant—a cook—and one ranch foreman overseeing four cowboys.

Howdy started back in the late afternoon but soon realized that he was far from being a seasoned horseman. He stopped at the water's edge to adjust his underwear that had begun to ride up. Howdy needed to sit on a patch of grass he hoped would be an improvement over a leather seat of torture. The horse nibbled on some grass, so Howdy dropped the reins and stretched before relaxing for a few minutes. Howdy located a dry swale of down sloping grass and plopped down. He'd take a few minutes siesta and then walk the beast back home.

When Howdy awoke it was getting dark, and his steed was gone. Muttering to himself how he was going to have to be more responsible, Howdy walked in the direction where he thought Asa's house should be. When he finally arrived, Howdy found everyone had retired for the evening. He climbed the stairs and heard giggles and whispered snippets coming from under Sydney's door. Howdy continued down the hall to Asa's room.

After a few light knocks, Asa poked his head out. He said, "I'm glad you made it back. Your horse got back around dark. Wilkins sent a rider to find you and hasn't yet made it back. Shall we take a brandy in the garden? But first tell me what happened."

"Not much to tell. I got off the horse to stretch, and the horse went home while I was stretching and not watching."

In the garden, the two men sat beside a trellis of fragrant flowers.

"So Asa, why does this spot smell like we've fallen into a bottle of french perfume?"

"Because the flowers on these vines bloom at night and they have to attract the bees and other pollinators by smell rather than bright ornamentation."

"Darn."

"What ever is the matter, Howdy?"

"Well, here we are in a scented garden, next to our feet lays a beautiful lake shimmering in the moonlight, and the stars are so bright I can make out the spirals in the Milky Way."

"Yes, it is beautiful."

"And I haven't got a pretty young thing to wrap my arms around or to quote poetry to."

"It seems that is your fault. You might not be able to handle my defiant sister, but either one of her two friends would jump at the chance to listen to you elucidate the mysteries of the universe in rhyming verse. Shall I go fetch one for you? Patricia perhaps?"

"No. I have to stay focused. I am your only hope and what I do for you will someday pay me dividends."

"I knew it. You're after something."

"No, not really. I just think you act before thinking things through and, when I weigh the pleasures of what I am doing without against the pain you could accidentally inflict on yourself, I find the scales tipped in your favor."

"My great-grandfather Albert had a friend like you. My father says he listened to stories the old man told about the troubles he and his best friend, Woodrow, tried to overcome. You see all this property? Our family fortune includes this house and furnishings, three hundred acres of land, and a bank. Do you have any idea how my family came to have such an abundance of wealth?"

"I haven't given it much thought."

"Well, Howdy, they didn't make it here. My great-grandfather struck gold in California. He was an adventurer and when word came there was gold in the California mountains he and Woodrow were logging timber in Washington. They sold their equipment and joined the migration. But the work was hard so, after working their staked mine for four months and having a paltry two small pouches of gold flakes and tiny nuggets, they salted their claim and sold it for ten times what it was worth.

"Albert and Woodrow were flim-flam artists—my great-grandfather more so than Woodrow. But at this point in their careers this was the most money they had ever accumulated. And it struck them that people were in a feeding frenzy with some having money. So Albert and Woodrow staked another claim and purchased a set of scales. They used the scales to pay other miners for their findings and then Albert and Woodrow used the purchased gold to salt their new mine, then sold it for another passel of money and headed farther up the canyon.

"Two years later they had to leave California because there were a bevy of people looking for them wanting their money back. At that time, in lawless California, it was common for people with similar grievances to form a lynch mob and get their brand of justice.

"Albert and Woodrow got out just in time, taking two horses, one pack mule, and two saddlebags stuffed with money and gold. According to my dad, his grandfather said it was a close call with them sneaking out in the middle of the night and leaving all of their equipment and most of their clothing.

"They zigzagged east trying to elude any pursuers. It wasn't until they reached Arkansas that they felt safe."

"So your great-grandfather Albert bought this piece of property and . . ."

"No, Albert wanted to keep going, so they stopped under a spreading live oak and counted their money. Albert kept the mule and half the money and went on to Georgia."

"Woodrow ended up marrying a woman and settled down. He vowed he'd never work again. Not that he had worked that hard before, but I guess the running was what he was meaning or maybe conning people out of their hard-earned money might have been it."

"So how did your family get here from Georgia?"

"Great-grandfather was a gambler and, with all his money, he played poker most nights. One night he passed out drunk after winning a big hand and woke up the next morning in an alleyway with broken ribs. All of his money had been stolen.

"Great-grandfather Albert wrote Woodrow to tell him what had happened. A couple of weeks later Woodrow showed up at the boarding house where Albert was staying, and the two of them went looking for Albert's poker playing companions. I don't exactly know what happened next, but Albert told my dad that Woodrow beat up one man so bad that the man was never right after the fight, another man was killed in a gunfight, a third was found dangling from a tree, and the fourth showed up at the boarding house asking if he could possibly give Albert his money back. Woodrow loaded all of Albert's stuff and hauled him back to Arkansas. And then Great-grandfather Albert bought this piece of land from Woodrow."

"Is Woodrow still alive?"

"No. He died almost fifty years ago. Dane, his only child, was born when Woodrow was an old man and Dane's daughter, Beatrice, is Woodrow's granddaughter."

"Asa, there is no way you're getting out of marrying that woman—nor should you want to."

"Howdy, you don't know the half of it yet."

CHAPTER 6 – THE PARTY

December, 1926

Howdy sat on a sturdy wrought-iron chair on his balcony to watch cars pull into the circular drive bringing one debutante after another to Asa's welcome home party. The drivers were told to return at midnight to pick up their charges.

Howdy learned that Asa was the only high school graduate from the 1923 Skunk Hollow graduating class who had started college. There were a lot of mothers in the area who had determined that the most eligible man in the county was also the most likely candidate for their daughter's hand. Trish, Lucy, and Sydney Rene coordinated the entire affair with Asa's father, Burris Thompkins, footing the bill.

The front of the house was lit with flickers of light extending several inches above the rims of painted gourds mounted on tall poles. The arriving girls wore evening dresses with each doing her best to make a memorable entrance from the car. Both front doors were open with servants standing guard. Wilkins announced each young lady when she arrived. Single men were also announced but with much less fanfare.

When Beatrice arrived, Howdy could see there was some small scene playing out when the servant opened the car door and escorted Miss Baxter through the front door. Howdy couldn't tell what was going on but surmised it had something to do with the way Beatrice was dressed. She wasn't wearing an evening dress like the other women but a red and white checked blouse. Its tails tied together above a wisp of a skirt. And Beatrice's black hair was braided in pig-tails.

Howdy adjusted his tie and headed down the stairs at a fast clip to see if he could head off a confrontation. When he got to the bottom of the stairs, Sydney Rene was laughing, with Lucy and Trish stifling giggles. Beatrice stood before them. She had tears sliding down her cheeks.

Sydney Rene said, "I'm sorry Beatrice. We changed the theme for the party, and I guess, we forgot to send you a notice. But, really, you look adorable."

Howdy approached the four women and said, "Beatrice, would you allow me to escort you into the ball-room. Sydney has set up a punch-bowl, and there are tidbits of food available."

"Thank you, Howdy. You are such a gentleman. Has Asa made an appearance yet?"

"No."

As they walked to where a small band could be heard tuning their instruments, Howdy said, "Beatrice, look at this like it's a trial to see if you can keep your composure while the other girls make fun. Every woman here has nightmares like the one you're in and, when it becomes apparent that you are a strong woman who is the master of any situation, they'll start switching to your side and applaud your ability to handle your misfortunes. And, Beatrice, I'll be right here to help."

"Oh, Howdy. You are a true friend."

Asa put his arm around Beatrice's shoulder. "Howdy would you bring Beatrice and me something to drink?"

"Sure." Howdy had to hurry. He had to find Wilkins and then to talk to Patricia—alone—and, of course, he had to deliver two glasses of punch to Asa and Beatrice.

Wilkins stood by the door. Howdy said, "Wilkins, my good man, I need two cowboy hats and three brightly colored scarves. Right now, Wilkins. This situation Sydney has caused with the Baxter girl will only get worse unless Asa and I can come to her rescue."

"Yes, sir. I'll need four minutes."

Howdy headed to the band conductor. "Sir, there has been a calamity. The person of honor thought you gentlemen would be playing a country hoe-down. If you could package in a few pieces in that genre or, maybe, some honky-tonk music, I'll make sure you get a generous bonus."

"Yes, sir. That's the music our guitar player loves to play."

"The first piece on my cue. And the more you can come up with the bigger the bonus."

Howdy saw Patricia standing alone. He motioned for her to meet him at the stairs while he sloshed two dippers of punch into two crystal cups, and found Wilkins. "You give those to me and take these two glasses to Asa and Beatrice."

At the stairs he removed his tie, positioned one Stetson on his head, and asked Patricia if she would tie one of the bandannas around his neck. When she had finished and had deftly dropped Howdy's tie into her purse, he picked up the remaining hat and one of the two remaining bandannas. Howdy walked at a brisk clip to where he had left Asa and Beatrice.

Howdy handed Asa the second Stetson and bandanna. "Put these on, and don't ask questions." He made a motion to the band leader and turned to Beatrice. "Milady, may I have the pleasure of your granting me this dance?"

"Howdy, I'm not going to dance in this outfit to . . ."

The band started cranking out something by Hank Williams. Howdy gave a wink to Beatrice and led her to the floor. For the next four minutes Howdy pushed, pulled, and twirled Beatrice around the floor. After the dance was over Howdy took Beatrice back to Asa and gave him a glare that Asa took to mean 'You better jump in here buddy or you can kiss managing the bank good-bye.'

The next dance was to a Roy Acuff country standard. While Asa and Beatrice sashayed around the floor, Patricia walked over and stood beside Howdy. She was now wearing a large red bandanna around her neck.

"So, embarrassing Beatrice was the big secret?"

"Part of it. I'm now quite distressed at our childish behavior. Uh oh, here comes the rest of it."

Howdy looked around the room. Wilkins was escorting a young lady wearing a pretty rose-red evening gown. It was smooth, clinging to her body from a strapless top clear to the floor.

Wilkins waited for the song to end then said, "Ladies and gentlemen, Miss Isabelle Fontane."

For a brief moment, the room grew quiet as everyone appraised the woman who had just arrived. Then it returned to light conversations coming from small groups of people. Asa looked rattled as Isabelle made her way to where he stood beside Beatrice. Howdy grabbed Patricia by the hand and walked her straight into a viper's den.

Beatrice was polite but uneasy. She was keenly aware of the striking difference between her hairstyle and the clothes she was wearing with the formal eveningwear Isabelle was wearing. When Howdy and Patricia walked up Asa was stammering.

"Howdy, there you are. Let me introduce you to Isabelle Fontane. Miss Fontane, this is my best friend, Howdy Monroe."

Isabelle held out her hand. "Pleased to meet you, Mr. Monroe."

"Just call me Howdy." He touched the front brim of his cowboy hat. Were you a 'Polecat' like Asa?"

"For three years. He sat behind me in social studies and was my lab partner in biology."

"I see. And now?"

"And now, I work at his father's bank."

Asa said, "She'll be working for me in a couple of years. Dad said he would start me out cleaning the ashtrays and mopping the floors. That he'd gradually work me up into more important positions. I figure a year or two of hard work before I take over."

"Will you have time for travel?" Beatrice asked.

"When I'm totally in charge I can take off when I please. Dad now takes a month every summer to go fishing in Montana."

Isabelle said, "Have you ever been to New York City? I've always wanted to walk down Fifth Avenue, to buy something at Bloomingdales, to see a play."

"No. Never have."

The band started playing a Jo Stafford ballad. Beatrice said, "Asa, let's dance. I feel like holding you in my arms."

"Howdy turned to Patricia. "Do you know the words?"

"I do, but you don't have enough money to bribe me into singing them."

"Maybe not to the entire crowd but just to me. I'd make it worth your while."

"If we were dancing I wouldn't mind singing in your ear."

Howdy turned to see Asa and Beatrice head to the dance floor, and Isabelle walk to a group of people cornering a scared punchbowl. "Patricia, may I have the honor of this dance."

"I'd be delighted."

In a few minutes people were leaving the dance floor, some were waiting for the next tune, Beatrice was looking for the ladies' room, and Asa was looking for Isabelle.

To Patricia, Howdy said, "So you three girls were looking to stir up trouble by putting Beatrice on the defensive with an entirely wrong set of clothes and putting Asa in a no win situation with two women wanting his attention. You know, of course, Asa is an unsuspecting prey to a conniving alley cat named Isabelle and a petulant, spoiled daddy's girl named Beatrice. They both have agendas planned for the next Skunk Hollow bank manager."

"It was all Sydney Rene's idea. She wants her dad to hold off grooming Asa to take over while she figures a way for him to consider her."

"Patricia, you're a better woman than what that situation called for."

"I am? Well yes, I am. However, I'm more than a little embarrassed that you had to point it out."

Beatrice walked up and asked, "Have either of you seen Asa? He was going to wait for me."

Both Howdy and Patricia looked in the direction of the punch bowl for a glimpse of rose-red. No such luck. Howdy said, "You two ladies stay right here while I go look for him."

Howdy left in a hurry. He had to find Wilkins.

Both ladies headed to the punch bowl. After a few minutes of silence Beatrice said, "I bet I know where he is. He says that when he needs a moment of peace he likes to go into the library. Let's go there to see if all the excitement has driven him to his safe place."

"No. I think we should wait on Howdy."

"Nonsense. You can wait if you want, but I'm heading to the library."

"Okay, okay, if you have to go, I'll tag along."

"Wilkins, have you seen Asa?" asked Howdy.

"Have you checked the library? I saw Miss Fontane slipping in just a few moments ago."

"Was she with Asa?"

"Mr. Howdy, that I do not know. But she was looking over her shoulder, and the door was only open wide enough for her to step through side-ways."

"Wilkins, point me in the right direction. We got a situation happening."

"Mr. Howdy, go through those double doors and turn left. It'll be the second door on your right."

Howdy ran through the doors only sliding to a stop when he spied Patricia standing in the hall looking through the door he had been mapped to. Howdy hurried the next twenty feet. Patricia stepped to the side so he could see inside.

Asa stood in the middle of the room with Isabelle hiding behind. Beatrice was a predator stalking. She had both hands extended forward baring long sharp fingernails. Slowly edging around Asa, Beatrice emitted a low hissing sound. The hair on Howdy's neck stood up.

Howdy entered the room. Calmly he said, "Beatrice, get a grip, girl. The situation is not what you think. Asa was only showing her a few good books she could have for holiday reading."

"How could you believe that? She was sitting in his lap with her arms cradling his head."

"Were they doing anything?"

"They were kissing."

"Was Isabelle kissing Asa?"

"Yes, she was."

"Okay, Beatrice, they came in the library to get a few books and Isabelle cornered him. He wasn't kissing her she was the instigator he was only being a gentleman. Isn't that right, Asa."

"I . . . uh . . . I don't know what happened. It sure isn't what it looks like, Beatrice, honey. You can't believe everything you see. Uh . . . Isabelle and I are only good friends.

At this bit of information, Isabelle pounded Asa's back with both fists. "You jerk. As soon as I got through the door you had your hands on me dragging me to that chair."

"Now, Isabelle."

"Now, Isabelle nothing. Asa Thompkins, we are through. I'm not going to sneak around with you behind Beatrice's back anymore.

Howdy, have Mr. Wilkins call my ride. I'm going home. As for you, Beatrice, you can have him." Isabelle left the room in a huff.

"Asa, I have lived my entire life thinking you and I would marry someday. But no more."

CHAPTER 7 – THE PAWN
November, 1930

Burris Thompkins ordered an impromptu meeting of his bank's Board of Directors. Danger was in the air.

Paul Eversole, Jim Strake, Gladys Moore, and Hamilton Thompkins were seated around a long, massive oak table when Dane Baxter arrived. Burris was nervously twitching a pencil and looking out a window.

"Good, we're all here. Dane would you like something to drink before we get started?"

"No. I'm fine."

Burris pulled back his chair at the head of the table and plopped down. "I don't think anyone is aware of what happened in Kentucky today. The reason I thought we should get to together is to decide a plan of action if the same thing happens here."

"What happened in Kentucky?" asked Gladys.

"There was a run on the National Bank of Kentucky."

Gladys said, "And you think the same thing is going to happen here?"

"It's inevitable. By this afternoon, other banks all over Kentucky were having similar problems. It'll soon spread to other states. I've read that America has more than twenty-five thousand banks operating under fifty-two different regulatory regimes. Most of them small rural affairs like ours. Carter Glass, father of the Federal Reserve System, has said on record that, 'The majority are no more than pawnshops often run by little corner grocery-men calling themselves bankers.' He added that, 'All they know is how to shave a note.'" Burris paused a moment and looked around the room at his small ineffective group of board members. "Small, rural banks have had to lock their doors at a rate of five hundred per year for the entire decade of the twenties. Six hundred and fifty-nine closed in twenty-nine. This year through last month we have already surpassed the total for last year, and we have two more months to go. Almost all of the closed banks were small and in rural areas of the country, but the National Bank of Kentucky was the largest bank in their state. So the number of bank foreclosures has increased, and it now has spread to large banks in urban financial centers. It's not financially healthy to be a banker, a small banker, a small rural banker in the United States. And the situation is worsening. What we have to decide today is what we should do if our depositors rush through the front doors wanting their money.

Dane Baxter said, "How liquid are we Burris?"

"We can handle a small rush, but if something like what happened in Kentucky happens here, we'll go under."

"Is there anything we can do?"

"Yeah. I've been putting a plan of action together in my head, and I thought I'd run it by the board to see if you approve.

"First, we ought to cash in any federal bonds we have and sell the stocks in our portfolio.

"Second, we need to call in any loans where the borrower is behind more than two payments.

"And Third—and this is the hardest one of all—we have to foreclose on the collateral pledged by anyone who can't bring their obligation into a current status."

Dane was deep in thought. He had cash in a safe at his house. If the bank foreclosed and auctioned off the collateral, there would be bargains to have. And he'd pay for his purchases with the money he had on deposit first before dipping into his stash. He raised his hand. "I propose that we put the plan as you have explained it into action as soon as possible."

Jim Strake said, "I second the motion."

Burris asked for a vote, and the motion carried unanimously. "I will keep everybody informed if any new developments come up. If there is no other business, this meeting stands adjourned."

The next day Burris drove to the Baxter ranch. He found Dane in the barn tending a sick heifer. "Good morning, Dane."

"You're not bringing bad news are you? You don't have a line at the bank clamoring for their money do you?"

"No. Nothing like that. I just came over to ask, if we needed emergency funds are you in a position where you could help?"

"I'd have to receive something in return."

"Like?"

"Three things. I'd have to feel reasonably sure you'd pay the money back. That Asa and Beatrice marry."

"Now Dane, Beatrice is the one who called off the marriage—not Asa."

"Yes, but it was because she caught that boy of yours kissing another woman, and your daughter embarrassed her at Asa's party. Burris, can you not keep your kids in line?"

"Okay. Okay. So what's the third condition?

"That is just a bit of information, and you can give that to me after the you meet the first two conditions, and while I'm dangling a hundred thousand just above your greedy paws."

"Information? What kind of information?"

"Don't worry. You'll not go to jail or anything. Just take care of the first two conditions and the third will be easy."

"Dane, there is nothing about you that is easy. But I'll do my best. By the way what would be the best way for me to assure you that you'll get your money back?"

"Give me something of yours to hold that's worth the money. I can allow you a full year to pay me back."

"Like a pawn."

"Yep."

CHAPTER 8 – ASA IN PARIS

December, 1930

Asa stepped off the train and into the waiting arms of a city alive with energy. The city of lights. The city of love. But he was at a disadvantage. He didn't know his way around this beautiful city, and he didn't speak French.

Asa asked a taxi driver in English to take him to the Hotel Deville but the man didn't understand so Asa looked through a French phrase book and spent five minutes trying to make the cab driver understand his destination. The man muttered a few undecipherable words, looked at Asa with contempt, and shirked his shoulders each time Asa said something while looking at the taxi driver for an indication of understanding.

Asa was about to find another driver when the location of Hotel Deville struck a chord. The man excitedly spoke a few words that included the hotel name Asa wanted transportation to. The cab driver said, "Oui" and loaded Asa's two suitcases into the trunk of the car.

From a front pocket, Asa removed several bills of the French currency he had received at one of the exchange counters inside the train station. Paris was a large city, and its streets were full of cars. Just like every other large city Asa had ever been in, the taxis did not feel constrained by traffic laws nor concerned with the safety of any slow-moving pedestrian. Asa was extremely happy when the cab pulled up to the Hotel Deville. The cab driver opened his trunk and held out his hand.

"That'll be ten francs for you and two more for each suitcase."

"This would have been so much more pleasant if you had owned up to speaking English."

"Pleasant for who? It was fine with me." The cab driver took the sixteen francs and said. "If you English would tip better you'd get better service."

"I'll keep that in mind."

Howdy was sitting beside a pretty lady and conversing in fluid French when Asa walked up dragging two suitcases. Howdy jumped up then said something to the young lady who promptly opened her purse and handed Howdy a card. Howdy kissed the back of her hand and took his leave from the pretty woman. When he reached Asa, he took one of the two suitcases.

"Asa, I'm so glad to see you. Do you not speak French?"

"No. My foreign language was Mexican."

"Ha, ha. You mean Spanish."

"No. It was Mexican."

"Okay. Let's get these bags to the room, and we'll go to the bar to discuss our strategy."

"How have you been, Howdy. I know we men are not known for abundant letter writing, but two or three letters a year from you is an abysmal effort."

"I know, Asa. I'm sorry about that. You've been better than me at the letter writing, but it might be that there is more going on in your life than in mine. For me, I'm still working for the Bank of England. No, that's not true. I told them that a friend of mine was coming into town, and I wanted to take a few days off. My despicable boss said I had used all my available leave when I went home to visit my parents, and I wouldn't be given anymore until the start of the new year.

"Well, this was my last year, so I turned in my resignation and caught a plane here. I feel like I've just been let out of jail. Let's celebrate."

"Didn't they treat you well?"

"Oh yeah. The only one that was difficult was my immediate boss, and I think that's because he got the idea somewhere that I wanted his job."

"You didn't want it did you?"

"Good heavens no. But after overhearing him refer to me as 'the Colonial' I let him think I did."

"You could have written and told me about him."

"I see your point. But let's discuss Beatrice. Have you written any letters to her?"

"A few but no replies."

"That little episode with Miss Fontane has bitten you in the foot."

"Howdy, that little episode with Miss Fontane has done much more than that. My family told me to bring back Beatrice or not to come back."

"They were just kidding."

"I'd like to think they were, and did so until Dad sold my car. He said he'd hold off on the rest of my stuff to see how well I did in Paris. Howdy, if I go back empty handed I'll have to get a job just to eat."

"Then you are truly going to marry this woman to keep your assets and an easy way of life."

"Yep."

"Did you bring much money? Paris is an expensive city."

"Tell me about it. My taxi fare from the train station to the hotel was a half week's salary. Just the tip was a day's wages. And the cab driver berated me for being parsimonious when determining the amount."

"Asa, it's just money. Look at it like it's an investment. Beatrice will be so happy to see you that we might have to ask her to hold her horses while we get to see the town. Then you can go home to a hero's welcome and start mending fences with your family and hers."

At the bar the young lady Howdy had been sitting beside when Asa arrived, walked up to Howdy and gushed her pleasure at seeing him again. She said she'd be right back and for Howdy not to leave then dashed off with a grinning smile. At least that was what Howdy told Asa she had said. In a few minutes, she brought a much older man. From what Asa could make out the young lady had gone after her father, and from the way Howdy was squirming, there was some angst accumulating in the older man's demeanor.

After being caught off his guard, Howdy regrouped and started to gain a foothold on the situation and after another ten minutes of intense negotiation the old man seemed mollified, his daughter mortified, and Howdy relieved.

"What was that all about?"

"Asa, you could learn something from that exchange. It seems, in matters of love, women are more susceptible to flattering innuendos than men. A casual remark to a man is dismissed as hyperbole, and a similar remark to a woman is a proposal.

"Asa, what was the reason for Beatrice coming to Paris in the first place?"

"I'm not sure. She's almost two years younger than me and had finished high school the year before. She always thought of herself as being a little provincial. Maybe she came out here to get away from our country influence. A woman has to feel good about herself before she can come to grips with serious problems in her life. Maybe she came here to see a larger picture. You know to place a person's view of themselves, their problems, their achievements—or lack of achievements—in a proper perspective."

"What kind of problems could a young, pretty woman like Beatrice have?"

"Psychological. She never thought she was good enough. She cried quite a bit and for the flimsiest of reasons. If you hadn't been at that party to bolster her spirit with those cowboy hats and bandannas, she might have had a meltdown. Sydney Rene wasn't aware of her delicate psyche or she wouldn't have tested the waters like she did."

"Well, I wish you'd told me. I could have been more compassionate and more attentive to her needs."

"And that would not have helped me. As it was she was beginning to compare me with you, and I would have lost that battle. Howdy, you are so social. You don't have any problem talking with the ladies. I'm a wallflower compared with you."

"That's nonsense. Asa, you're tall, good-looking, and smart. And you have a bright future—everything a woman wants."

"Yeah. Let's put that on a sign, and let me wear it around so everyone will know."

"Okay, here's what we do. We'll requisition a second sofa for our room, and I'll conduct multiple counseling sessions. I'll get both of you feeling good about yourselves and then about each other and, while you are discussing that, I'll quietly leave the room, so the two of you can restore your amiable feelings for each other. Then we'll pack up and head back before either of you start to develop misgivings. What do you say?"

"I say that I will be better off talking to her by myself; without you distracting her with your boyish charm. I need you for support, but I don't want to have to compete with you. Is that all right, Howdy? I have a lot at stake here and don't want anything to go wrong."

"I completely understand, Asa. I'll stay in the background. You just let me know when I can help and what you need help with."

"You are a good friend, Howdy. Now I'd like to go up to the room for a good night's sleep so we can get an early start tomorrow.

"But before I see her I want to know as much as I can about her circumstances. So, I'll turn over to you that bit of . . . now what do accountants call that . . . let's see . . . ?"

"Due diligence."

"Yes. That's it. Howdy, you are responsible for gathering the information I need on Beatrice Baxter—the due diligence."

The next morning both men were up and dressed early. They left the hotel and crossed the street to a sidewalk café where they discussed their strategy and consumed multiple cups of espresso and ate a prodigious amount of pastries. Both men pushed away from the table.

Asa said, "I couldn't live here. I'd spend my days strung out on caffeine and be a hundred pounds overweight."

"I agree. From now on I'll order for you and you order for me."

"Sounds fair enough. But beware, I normally don't eat quite as many sweets as you and I drink my coffee black."

"But that's the secret of this game. I'm ordering for me, and you eat what you like of what I order and I'll do the same with what you order.

"When my parents moved from Cleveland to Phoenix, they went from a two story house with six thousand square feet to one half that size. I remember my dad trying to decide what he should pack and what to give to the church. He was having a hard time parting with anything. My mother was in the same boat, so they switched. My dad chose what my mother should pack, and she did the same for him.

"When it came to choosing the furniture that got to go, they took each room in the new house one at a time and each made a list of what to take for that one room. The only things that got to go were items listed on both sheets. Any furniture item listed on one sheet and not the other stayed. It worked marvelously well, but the church fared the best with a garage sale that set the high mark for all garage sales in our area of Cleveland."

"So, good buddy, you think you ordering for me and me for you will keep either one from gaining excess weight?"

"Let's give it a shot. We don't have anything to lose and might enjoy a little different cuisine."

"All right, Howdy. Here's Beatrice's address. Let's see what you can come up with, because tomorrow, I'm calling on her."

"Will you be okay on your own?"

"Now what kind of trouble can I get myself into? I'll stroll along the sidewalks, shop at some of the retail stores, and take a taxi back to the hotel when I get tired. We'll get back together tonight to discuss what you've found out."

Howdy first went to the United States Embassy where he checked on Beatrice's passport status. From a pretty, young clerk, Howdy used his boyish charm to find that Beatrice currently lived in a ladies boarding house, her telephone number, and that she had spent an entire year attending a French cooking school. Currently, she attended the Sorbonne University where she was taking courses in French history, aesthetics, and a survey of opera. And twice a week she received private voice instruction.

From there he went to the French government office for visas and found she had renewed her visa six times and currently held a part-time job at the French Museum of Fine Art.

Howdy made a hasty trip to the museum and found she was one of three lecturers who gave scheduled trips for groups of students who wanted an in depth and informative tour of the museum.

Howdy waited for her to return from one tour and to begin a second. He was in for a surprise. When Beatrice appeared, Howdy had to escape from the museum to find Asa as quick as he could.

Asa had spent the day shopping—more accurately just looking because he could not believe the prices. At a used book stall, he purchased a couple of books in English and caught a taxi back to the hotel.

Howdy ran to Asa. "I saw her. Asa . . . Asa, she's changed."

"How has she changed?"

"I don't know how to tell you this, Asa. Sir, you have a difficult job ahead of you. I almost didn't recognize her."

"Howdy, quit this beating around the bush. How has she changed? Why will I have a difficult job? And why did you not easily recognize her? She's Beatrice, Howdy. Beatrice!"

"You know Asa. I don't want to say anything about her looks just now but let me tell you what she's been doing with her time. She spent a full year learning the art of French cooking. She's been in France for almost four years and during the last three she's been attending one of the most prestigious universities in all of Europe. She's been taking courses in the French culture and the study of all things beautiful. And, besides taking courses at the Sorbonne, she has a job at the French Museum of Fine Art. She lectures students on the items they have on exhibit. And, Asa, she's taking private instruction at night for voice. Asa, the woman has changed. She isn't the Beatrice you knew three years ago, Asa. She is a new Beatrice, and I don't want to be held to my bargain with you anymore."

"You what?"

"That's right, Asa. I think she might be the woman for me, and then you can have Isabelle like you've always wanted."

"Howdy, what have you been drinking?"

CHAPTER 9 – THE REAL BEATRICE

December, 1930

Early the next morning Asa turned over and realized it was still in the pre-dawn hours with the city just now waking. A lighter sky appeared when looking east. He quietly slipped from under the covers, closed the heavy drapes, and stole into the bathroom. Thirty minutes later Asa emerged, cleanly shaved and bathed. With the curtains closed, the room was pitch black. Asa fumbled with his largest suitcase, decided on his attire by feeling the texture of each garment, and dressed the best he could without making noise.

Asa slowly opened the door, slid through sideways, and placed a Do-Not-Disturb sign over the door knob after pulling it closed.

Before catching a taxi, he walked across the street and purchased coffee and two pastries. Asa then gave the hotel doorman a slip of paper with Beatrice's address penciled in and gave him a decent tip after he hailed a taxi and gave the driver instructions.

When Asa arrived he was surprised to see Howdy drinking a cup of coffee, holding a bouquet of cut flowers, and leaning against Beatrice's boarding house. "Howdy, how did you beat me here? I left you still asleep—and where did you get those flowers?"

"I'm just looking out for my own best interests. I've been here for over an hour. You must have surmised the pillow I stuffed under the covers was me. And I had a taxi driver travel here by way of the flower district. Asa, did you not get enough sleep? You look terrible. Is that a rash on your face?"

"Howdy, you do realize that Beatrice is my girlfriend?"

"Asa, when I saw Beatrice yesterday I decided that she was too much woman for you. She needed someone who would appreciate her for who she was. And that is not as a meal ticket. I can give her all the things she wants, all the things she needs, and you can't. No, for you, she is only a present to throw at your father's feet. And, as for her being your girlfriend, well that just isn't so. The last thing I heard her say four years ago was that the two of you were through."

"Yes, well that was just an unfortunate misunderstanding."

"I guess we'll soon find out if Beatrice still feels the same way or if she has moved on."

"Howdy, I'll give you ten dollars for those flowers."

Before Howdy could answer, the front door opened and Beatrice stood in the opening. She carried a large leather satchel under a blue cape and wore a matching beret.

"My goodness. Today has just started and is already full of surprises. I never expected to see you again, Asa, or you, Howdy. Whatever are the two of you doing in Paris?"

Asa stammered, "Uh . . . ah, we've come to see you, Beatrice."

"And to tell you how much we've missed you, Beatrice." Added Howdy.

"I'm flattered. But I have school this morning and have to work in the afternoon. Maybe we could have dinner somewhere this evening."

Howdy said, "I'll get us a taxi."

"No, that won't be necessary. After school, I have to work at the museum."

"I could be at your school with another taxi to take you to the museum and then later at the museum to bring you home," said Howdy.

"With me," added Asa.

Howdy held out the flowers. "You look magnificent, Beatrice. These are for you."

"You're so sweet, Howdy. Always saying and doing the right things. Asa must be proud to have a friend like you."

"Not so much lately."

"Whatever do you mean, Asa?"

"Well, that's between Howdy and me."

"And me. Howdy's my friend too."

"Beatrice, I want to be more than a casual friend. I think after you and Asa have had a chance to catch up on old times you should send him on his way, and you and I could take up where Asa was reluctant to go."

"This is certainly a turn of events. Howdy, I don't know what to say. Asa, do you have any comment?"

"Beatrice, I'm sorry for the way I've treated you. I never saw Isabelle again after the party. And I didn't realize how much I loved you until you made it quite clear we were through. I'd like a second chance."

"And, Howdy, you'd like a first chance?"

"That's right."

"Let me put these flowers in water. I'll be right back. If Henri arrives to pick me up, tell him I'll be right out."

"Henri?"

"Yes, he's my boyfriend."

Beatrice had just stepped inside when a car drove up with a man jumping out and running to Beatrice's front door. He rang the bell."

"Pardon me, are you Henri?"

"Yes."

"Beatrice said she'd be right out."

"That woman. She knows I can't be late."

"If you need to, you're welcome to go ahead. We can deliver Beatrice after she finishes whatever she's doing. She said it would only be fifteen minutes or so."

"Thanks, tell her I'll meet her at the Student Union after first period."

"Don't mention it."

The man ran to his car and drove off waving out the window.

"What do you think, Howdy?"

"I think Henri is thirty years old—maybe older than that."

"That's what I was thinking. What do we do now?"

CHAPTER 10 – LOVE ME. NO ME.

December, 1930

As the evening approached Asa and Howdy still had not reconciled their differences with each getting dressed and mumbling incoherently about the other's shortcomings. On Beatrice's doorstep Howdy shoved Asa off the concrete steps when Beatrice opened her door, but it was Asa who managed to open the car door for Beatrice and slide in beside her while Howdy had to run to the other side.

Howdy paid the taxi and then grabbed the unoccupied arm of Beatrice so they could enter the Moulin Rouge three abreast. It was Howdy that tipped the Matre d' so they'd have a table convenient to the stage for the performance after the meal. Behind Beatrice's back, they agreed that Howdy would make all of the financial arrangements with the two of them settling up after the evening was over.

From the wine list, Howdy picked an acceptable chardonnay while Asa and Beatrice studied the dinner menu. Asa was having difficulty. He even turned the menu upside-down hoping it would make better sense from another angle. When the waiter came for their selections, Beatrice was the first to order and did so in perfect French. The waiter turned to Asa, who took a drink of water while pointing to an entry. The waiter then turned to Howdy.

"I'll have the *Tartar de Legumes et Soup de Pointes Vertis, Salad d'Herbes Fraiches*. And for the main course bring the *Filet de Boeuf Rouge, Poelee de Grenailles au Thym, Haricots Verts au Beurre Frais, Sauce au poivre*."

The waiter looked at Howdy's glass of chardonnay.

Howdy responded with, "And a glass of the house, red *Bordeaux*."

"*Oui, Monsieur*."

Beatrice started the conversation with, "Howdy, I think you ordered the specialty of the house. You should enjoy it. And, Asa, what did you order?"

"I'm not sure. I could only read the prices so picked something reasonable and pointed to it."

"I see."

Howdy moaned, "No you don't see. Not yet. Asa and I made this arrangement where I would eat whatever he ordered, and he would do the same for my selections."

"So, Asa, you should enjoy your meal and Howdy, you are in for a surprise."

Asa said, "Beatrice, I suppose you have been here before. What kind of entertainment can we expect?"

"Yes, I've been here once or twice. A small band plays background music for an hour or so and then an MC comes out and introduces the band and the dancers. They perform a number of tunes accompanied by choreographed dancing. With the music getting louder and more raucous and the dancing more frenzied and more enthusiastic as time passes. They finish in a flourish with the *Can Can*."

"I can tell we are not in Arkansas anymore."

Beatrice said, "Asa, we have fun in Arkansas. Our bands there have guitars, fiddles, and harmonicas and the dancing is not exactly precision, but it is entertaining, and it's what the people want to see and do. Paris is just a different culture and the people here have their own preferences. One is not better than the other—just different."

The waiter brought out a large tray held above his head and, while a cohort opened a napkin for Howdy and Beatrice, he placed salad plates and soup tureens before each.

Howdy looked at his herbal salad and bowl of green asparagus soup before passing it to Asa. Beatrice took a small fork to spear snails she found lurking in shells. The waiter dripped a vinaigrette salad dressing on her accompanying green leafy salad.

Asa apologized. "I guess I didn't order a salad or soup, Howdy. I'm sorry."

"Don't worry about it, Asa. That was a chance I took when we made the agreement."

Between bites Beatrice said, "Neither of you has told me what you're doing here."

Since Asa's mouth was full, Howdy said, "We've come for you, Beatrice."

"Is that right, Asa?"

"Yeah." Asa took another bite. "Howdy, this is so good."

"And why do the two of you want me to come back?"

Asa wiped his mouth with a corner of his napkin before saying, "Because we—I love you. And I'm ready to get married."

"And you, Howdy?"

"Uh, I'm not quite ready to get married yet, but I'd like a chance to get to know you better, and marriage is certainly a possibility. I'd like for you to come to Arizona to meet my parents. We should spend some time together to see how compatible we are and, if everything worked out, we'd get married and move into a small apartment in Austin. You could get a job to help pay the bills until I graduated with my masters degree."

"And Asa, do you already have a job?"

"I do. If you marry me, Dad has promised I could work for him at the bank and be on the fast track to managing it by myself."

"Those are two good choices. One to marry a man with a good job who got that job by marrying me, but I'd be living close to my parents. And choice number two would be marrying a charismatic man who talks a good game, but leaves a girl wondering how sincere he is. A handsome man with unlimited potential but not quite sure of his timing. A third choice would be to continue living here on my own, making my money, and dating—or maybe marrying, Henri. By the way, he has also proposed. Henri's family lives on France's southern coast and want me to move there when Henri finishes his degree and starts his medical internship."

"You can't do that Beatrice; I need you." Asa was wringing his napkin.

"Asa, your dad won't give you the bank until you marry me. It's always been my ace in the hole. But that's not the kind of relationship I want. Not now. With that kind of basis it would not be many years before you would be looking for a more satisfying relationship and I would have to be constantly watching you to see who you would like to replace me with. And you, Howdy. You are a puzzle. I don't know if you love me or you are trying to help your buddy out of a bad predicament. What I do know is that Henri loves me for who I am with no strings attached. Right now he's the leading contender. But I'll hold off making my choice known while I gather more evidence. I have to make the best and smartest decision."

The waiter came by with another platter held above his head. After placing the platter on a portable support, he cleared away the salad plates and soup tureens and replaced with three round covered dishes. Then with a flurry he removed each cover much to the approval of each diner—except for Howdy, who had kept his eyes closed expecting the worst.

Beatrice was presented with a chicken breast surrounded with steaming vegetables and covered with a creamy sauce containing small onions and wild mushrooms. In front of Howdy, the waiter placed a plate displaying several small beef medallions covered in an orange pepper sauce. It also held small fried potatoes with twigs of thyme and French green beans covered with a buttery cheese sauce.

In front of Asa, the waiter placed a large bowl. It produced a cloud of steam when the cover had been removed. Asa took a spoon to poke around in the liquid to see what ingredients might be hiding. Asa lowered his head to smell and promptly held the bowl aloft so it could be exchanged for the exotic slices of beef in the orange pepper sauce given to Howdy.

Beatrice looked in Asa's bowl and said, "I think this is *Riz de Veau.*"

"And that is . . . ?"

"Veal thalamus glands. I've never tried it but heard the meat is tender. Howdy, you might like it. Have you ever tried sweetbreads?"

"No."

"Well, what you ordered for me is wonderful. And, again I apologize for the disgusting menu item I pointed to." Asa put another bite into his mouth.

Howdy shifted gears. "Beatrice, Christmas is in three weeks. When will your classes end?

"I have two more weeks, with my tests on the Thursday before Christmas Day."

"And will that also end college for Henri, with him leaving for the southern coast of France? And hoping to have you going with him?"

"Yes."

"And he will be expecting an answer by then?"

"Yes."

"Asa, if you can take a minute away from my food, it looks like we have a little less than three weeks to make Beatrice change her mind and come back to the states with one of us."

"We ought to be able to accomplish that."

"I don't know. I'm getting into the fray a little late and will have to work hard to make up for lost time. But then again I bet Henri will have to be spending his time studying and not minding the store. And you . . ." Howdy looked at Beatrice. ". . . are probably already prepared for your exams."

"Quite possibly."

"Then let me order the desserts while each of us plans a course of action to bring to fruition the fulfillment of our wildest desire."

CHAPTER 11 – BUILDING THE WIND
May, 1937

Luther squirmed in his seat. The banker had been looking at their proposal, their drawings, and their model from different angles for ten minutes. Ten minutes of torture. Luther and his two best friends were graduating from the University of Michigan's School of Engineering. They had designed a futuristic automobile and needed money to build a prototype. Their original model had been built of light-weight wood on a scale of fifteen to one. It was a project they had been assigned as graduate students in the master's program. The car was so artistically conceived, so masterfully constructed, so beautiful to look at that all three students received the highest marks in their graduating class for its production. Now they wanted to build a full-sized working rendition to market to an auto manufacturer for a grasping public.

The banker put down the papers. He looked at the three young men sitting in front of his desk and said, "Your proposal sounds interesting. But you'd have to prove to me somehow that this is not just a passing fancy never to see the light of day."

Luther cleared his throat. "Uh . . . what do you have in mind, sir?"

"Well, my son has been reading about the All American Soap Box Derby. If you were to build me a racer that would win a few races then I'd agree that you three gentlemen have talent and the bank would be willing to wager that you could, indeed, provide a profitable product. A product the Chicago International Bank of Commerce would be willing to provide you with the funds to bring to fruition. What do you say?"

"Sir, the rules say that any racer has to be built by the boy driving it."

"Well, I think we can get around a few rules. Besides, there is no way the racing authorities would know unless one of the three of you provided them with that information, and I would word the contract in such a way that that wouldn't happen."

"I think we can provide you with a racer that will win a few events."

"I think I'll need two racers: a red one and a blue one. That way if he wins and the derby officials take the racer to place on display he'll have another for his personal enjoyment."

"Would you be willing to front us enough money to purchase the materials?"

"How much?"

"Two hundred each."

The banker reached into his pocket and took out a checkbook. "Who do I make this to?"

Luther said, "Cash. We'll take it to a teller on our way out."

"All right to cash. I'll make it for five hundred so you gentlemen will have a little extra in case you need it and can finish the job with a superior coat of paint. On the hood paint a man's round face with puffed out cheeks. Have him blowing air and name them *The Wind I* and *The Wind II.*"

CHAPTER 12 – SPENCER'S PLAN
May, 1946

Spencer reached in and retrieved two eggs. He carefully placed them in a basket. Gathering the eggs was his last chore. He had already slopped the pigs and milked the Jersey heifer. Not so long ago his major concern was keeping a low profile at St Bartholomew's Holy Catholic Orphanage so the two nuns would not single him out for some onerous chore or difficult assignment. During the years he had lived there he and his sister, Millie, prayed that a family would take them into their home. They wanted to be part of a family again. Their prayers were answered last Christmas when everyone in the orphanage found homes. The entire town had opened its arms.

Doing a few chores was nothing to repay the love he and his sister had received. Still, he would have liked the opportunity to sleep a little longer. As Spencer walked back to the house, he thought about how someday he would be an engineer and design tall buildings. How he would determine the stress the foundation would have to withstand, how many inches the building could sway in the wind and still be safe, how the elevator would work, how the flow of traffic would stream visitors and workers through, and how the heating and ventilation system would warm and periodically replace the air.

Or maybe he would design bridges. He had read about workers dying while constructing the Brooklyn bridge. Scientists now believed it was the air pressure they were in while building the bridge's foundation. Spencer shook his head. So much responsibility. He knew that if he were actually to live his dream he would have to acquire sufficient knowledge to keep his workers safe. He'd have to go to one of the nation's best engineering universities.

How to get to a university was now his biggest worry. Through an article in yesterday's paper a plan started to develop. There he read an article about the All American Soap Box Derby. Officials were coming to Skunk Hollow to scope out the town's application to hold a local race. The race winner would travel to Akron, Ohio to compete with the winners of all the other local races across the United States. The ultimate winner would receive a paid scholarship to any state run university.

Spencer thought about standing up when his name was announced, to bow to the audience when the speaker said that he had won the 1947 All American Soap Box Derby. What would he say when asked which university he had chosen?

Spencer spent the rest of the day planning how he would get it done. He would go to the library to see if they had a book that had the soap box derby rules listed. He would then sketch out his racer, determine the materials needed for its construction, and put a purchase price on each part. Finally, he would tally the list so he would know how much it would cost to build.

Spencer whistled as he made his third trip into the kitchen that morning. The first was to wash his hands after slopping the pigs so he wouldn't foul the milk that was next on his list of chores. The second trip to the kitchen was to deliver the milk and get a basket for the eggs.

May was making biscuits when he handed her the eggs. Spencer started drawing his prototype at the kitchen table. May sneaked an occasional peek when she walked by or when she found Spencer so absorbed she thought he wouldn't mind.

"What you got there, honey?"

"The means to an end."

"The what?"

"May, you know how I've talked about building tall buildings. Of how I wanted to be an engineer. Well to fulfill my dream I need to graduate from a university and if I can build a fast soap box derby racer I might be able to do that without draining the family's savings."

"Spence, I hope you can do that because I'm not aware of any family savings. But what edge do you have over all of the racers being built by other boys?"

"I don't know, other than determination."

At the library, Nadine found three books with references made to the All American Soap Box Derby. Not one of the books had a list of the rules, but all three made general references that, lumped together, gave Spencer an indication of what was required. First the racer had to be built by a boy. He could get guidance or information on a particular problem to be resolved from an adult, but it was clear that experts could not build the racer.

Spencer also learned that the wheels and both axles had to be purchased from derby headquarters, that the total cost could not exceed a certain limit that varied from year to year, that the weight was limited to one hundred and fifty pounds or less, and with the driver could not exceed two hundred and fifty pounds. There were other rules like the distance the nose could stick out in front of the tires, what kind of braking system had to be installed, the steering configuration, and the seat had to be removable for inspection.

Spencer headed to the newspaper. He needed the address to write off for a derby entry application.

When Spencer opened the door to the *Marsden County Meteor,* he came face to face with an exciting and busy enterprise. People were hurrying from one place to another; three typewriters could be heard having their keys rhythmically pounded; a telephone ringing, then being answered; filing cabinet drawers opening and closing; people coming, going, and walking around him to get to where they were headed. Spencer was caught up in the excitement of putting out a paper.

"Young man, may I help you?"

Spencer broke out of his trance to reply, "I'd like to see Mr. Bell."

"Do you have an appointment?"

"Do I need one?"

"No. But you might have to wait until he has a free minute. May I tell him your name and what you've come to talk to him about?"

"My name is Spencer and I plan on winning the All American Soap Box Derby in Ohio. He and I have talked about other matters twice before. Tell him I'm Spencer."

"Have a seat, Spencer. Would you like a glass of water?"

"No. Thank you, ma'am."

"All right. I'll go tell him."

Spencer had waited ten minutes before the woman returned saying Mr. Bell would be with him shortly. After another ten minutes, she came back saying Mr. Bell asked for him to be patient he would not be much longer, then the man himself walked up and held out his hand.

"Spencer, I'm glad to see you. Midge tells me you're going to win the soap box derby."

"Yes, sir."

"Come into my office and we'll talk about it."

Back in Jesse Bell's private office, Jesse asked, "Now how may I be of assistance?"

"I need an entry application and a copy of the rules."

"I can get you both. But first, have you ever built anything like a racer before?"

"No."

"And yours will be faster than anyone else's because . . . ?"

"Because mine will be aerodynamically designed, have a low center of gravity, and be proportionally weighted."

"Holy cow! Spencer, you've got all the right words. But you'll have to work fast to develop the necessary skills. What are your plans to do that?"

"I don't have any yet. Do you have any ideas?"

"The best carpenters in the area are the two Calhoun brothers. Why don't you apprentice to them till time for school to start. Tell them what you want to do and see if they will teach you the skills."

CHAPTER 13 – REX
June, 1946

"I don't want to go to no stinking party. I won't know anyone there. I don't have a gift. And he didn't come to my birthday party, so why should I go to his?"

"Son, your birthday was back in January. We didn't live here then. And you have to make friends. Russell is your age. You and he will probably become good friends. Why don't you give it a shot? Consider it a gift to your father: the guy who buys you presents, takes you places, and puts up with your obstinate behavior."

"I'd want something in return."

"And what would that be that you don't already have?"

"A tree house."

"Rex, be reasonable. There is not a tree on our property that is big enough to hold a tree house."

"You'll have to think of something."

"There is a lot on Wexford street that has a sizable oak. What if I bought that lot and had someone build you a tree house. I could consider it an investment. Now, if someone came and offered me a decent profit for the lot we might have to move your tree house. Would you accept those terms?"

"If this first one was big enough—at least two rooms. And any replacement had electricity and running water."

"You want a tree house or a house stuck in a tree?"

"A tree house first and, if you want to sell it so you can make a profit, I want that profit spent on my next tree house."

"Son, have you thought about what kind of career you would like when you have to earn a living?"

"No. I've always thought you'd be there to give me what I wanted and if you weren't there you'd leave me enough that I wouldn't have to worry."

"That, my boy, is a sorry attitude. And being a banker might be just the ticket for someone with that kind of attitude."

"Those are my terms. We'll still have to get a present, but if you agree, then I'll go to the party. And I think being a banker would be boring."

"Okay, but we don't have time to buy anything. Let me go into the guest bedroom where we threw all our extra stuff. I'll find something in there. You can just hand it to him. No one would expect two men to be able to wrap a gift."

"That's all right with me as long as you don't give him anything of mine."

That afternoon Andy Muldoon dropped off his son at a local birthday party. They were a little late in arriving so no one was at the door to let the boy inside. Andy could hear noise coming from the back yard, so he and Rex walked around the house and entered the backyard through a wooden gate. Several boys were wearing tow sacks stretched to their chests and practicing their jumping.

Sydney Rene walked up to Andy holding out her hand. "So glad you and Rex were able to make it, Mr. Muldoon. We're getting ready for the sack race. Do you have time to help me officiate?"

"I suppose so. Just exactly what will I have to do?"

"Disqualify anyone who cheats and stand at the finish line with me and Asa to declare a winner."

"Asa, is here? So we have in attendance the Skunk Hollow Mayor and the largest single stockholder at my place of employment. I'll have to be on my guard."

"You needn't be worried Mr. Muldoon. Everyone is happy with your work at the bank. When Howdy came his one stipulation was that he be able to bring you. And now our assets have grown to an all time high."

"That makes me feel better. Is there somewhere I can put this trinket?"

"What is it you have there? Is that a plastic car?"

"Rex's cousin won the All American Soap Box Derby a few year's ago. This is a scaled replica of the racer he drove. He named it *The Wind*. It's numbered and signed."

"How delightful, Mr. Muldoon. May I call you Andy?"

When Rex entered the backyard, he could see that the people living there had money. There was a swimming pool and flowers had been planted everywhere. Several paths criss-crossed through the flower beds, with one crossing a small pond with flowers floating on a glassy top. In the distance, he could hear falling water.

Rex walked to a table and grabbed a tow sack. This party showed positive signs. If he had to attend he might as well have fun. Rex stepped into the tow sack and took a couple of jumps to see if he had a possibility of winning. There was no sense in participating if he couldn't win, so he took a few jumps to ascertain his chances.

Without looking to see exactly where he would be landing, Rex jumped onto a rock sticking out from a flower bed and fell. He wasn't hurt, but he did hear laughter aimed at his misfortune. During his scramble to get righted Rex spotted a green striped garter snake. Quick as a flash he had the snake in his grasp and now had to determine who laughed.

"Okay, everyone. Make your way to the starting line. Since most of the yard is made up of flower beds, the race will be one-time counter clock-wise around the swimming pool. We've drawn a starting and finishing chalk line across the concrete and through the grass to the closest flower bed. Each participant will have the choice of jumping the shortest distance, which is closest to the pool or the safest, which is in the yard.

"The winner gets two tickets to the circus coming to town in the fall and to step into the cage with the lion tamer. Wait a minute, we couldn't convince the lion tamer on that second prize. He thought the lions would not be able to perform with such a succulent dinner within easy reach. However, the two tickets are on the front row, and everyone knows that the front row at the circus is where the clowns play their pranks.

"Is everyone ready? On your mark. Get set. Wait a minute. This just in. We're adding a gift certificate of three dollars worth of candy from the Skunk Hollow Mercantile. Go." Sydney blew a loud whistle, and everybody was off in a dead earnest effort to win.

It wasn't but a minute until one boy strayed too close to the swimming pool and got pushed in. It wasn't apparent who did the pushing, but Andy noticed Rex was in close proximity. Then one boy jumped in on his own when he shouted there was a snake in his sack.

At one point, a boy fell and brought down five others with him. Rex was one of the boys who fell, and it infuriated him beyond measure. After getting to his feet, Rex found himself behind the leader by ten feet. When the leader crossed the finish line, Rex had almost caught up but he was definitely in second place.

"Okay, we have a winner." Sydney Rene walked over to a young man glowing red with pride. She held up his hand. "Our winner is Major Martin. There is one more game we'll be playing with like prizes. It's the three-legged race so spend the next hour or so finding a partner and planning your strategy. Major will be helping with the officiating since it would not be right for him to win both events."

"That was pretty exciting. Did you see that snake slither out of the sack and swim to the shallow end of the pool where he made it out and into the flower bed?"

Sydney Rene said, "I did. He didn't frighten me, but most of these boys have always lived in town and are afraid of snakes. They gave him plenty of room and time to make his escape."

During the next hour, the boys mingled with almost everyone paired. Usually, the paired boys were of similar heights, or similar weights, or of similar social status. Rex counted the possible participants and turned down two separate offers. He had to win the race and picking a partner that fit his strategy was of significant importance.

Hot dogs and lemonade were served with a few simple games like ring toss and croquet available to let the few girls in attendance an opportunity to participate.

When the last two boys paired up leaving only Rex without a partner, most boys thought Rex was upset for losing and had chosen not to race again. So it was a complete surprise when Rex loudly asked if there was not another boy for him to race with. When it was determined that there was not Rex asked Russell's sister if she would consider running as his companion. Lydia quickly answered in the affirmative. There were cries of deception as parents, other race participants, and other girls cried that it was not fair. Sydney finally decided that her daughter indeed could race. She knew girls could compete favorably with boys at most games. Then the girls in attendance also wanted to join in and asked the men for their belts. Andy gave his belt to a girl and a perplexed frown to Rex.

Rex asked Lydia to step over to a far flower bed where they could discuss their strategy without being overheard.

"Lydia, here's how we can win the race. You lean against my side with your arm around my waist. I'll walk briskly like you're not even there. You let your outside leg lightly touch the ground but don't put any weight on it."

"That's not necessary. I'm a strong girl. I can carry my own."

"Do you want to win or not?"

"Sure I want to win, but what I'm saying is that you think you have to win on your own and plan on dragging me along, and that's not the best way. The best way is to synchronize our steps. If you would reduce the length of your stride to thirty inches and we ran to a regular beat, both of us taking steps at the same time then we'd win without a struggle. I play clarinet in a marching band, and it's the beat that matters. For a race, it would just be a fast beat."

"So, you're saying that you could keep up with me no matter how fast I ran as long as I took 30 inch steps."

"And we tie our feet together at the ankle not at the knee. Also, you have to let me set the beat. We start off our first step with the inside foot and again when I say left. I'll gradually increase the beat until we're at a full run."

"Lydia, how'd you get to be so smart?"

"I take after my mom and she hates to lose or to come in second at anything to anybody."

"Okay, I'll agree but if we fall behind we go back to you hanging on and me in an outright run, because I want those tickets."

"If we win, and there are only two tickets, then you have to take me."

"I do? How old are you?"

"Eleven."

"Well, that's not going to work. I'm twelve, and I can't take someone still in elementary school."

"How bad do you want to win?"

"Awful."

"Is that 'awful bad' or 'this is just awful?'"

"Awful bad."

"All right. The two tickets Major won are next to the two tickets for winning this race so you give Major one of these tickets and he gives you one of his so that his two new tickets are still side by side and you and I have a ticket on either end of him and whoever he brings."

"Lydia, I may take you after all. I now see there are some things you are smarter about than me."

That afternoon Lydia and Rex won the three-legged race by twenty feet. Two girls came in second. The boys were astonished that they could be humiliated that way and vowed never to give the girls an equal chance ever again.

On the way home, Rex asked his dad, "Do you work for Russell and Lydia's mom?"

"In a way. My immediate boss is Howdy Monroe, and he answers to the stockholders. Lydia's mom owns more stock in the bank than any other person. Still she has to have other stockholders to vote their shares with her to get anything accomplished. The last I heard she owns twenty-seven percent of all outstanding stock."

"How much does Mr. Monroe own?"

"He told me that part of his salary is an option to buy stock but the quantity available varies on the profitability of the bank and restricted to what is in the company's treasury."

"All right, Dad. How do I become a banker?"

CHAPTER 14 – LAURIE

July, 1946

"Edwin, what do you want to do today?"

Edwin Stanky looked out the window from his wheelchair. What did he want to do? What were his possibilities? It was too hot to bathe in the thermal spring at City Park. He had been to Eudy's Drug and Fountain so many times he had started to gain weight. Laurie and Issie had taken him to watch the construction at the ballpark until it had been completed, and now it was too hot in the middle of the day to be out and about anyway.

"Well."

"I'm thinking." Edwin had been talking for about a month. It took him a half year of healing to recuperate well enough he could communicate his wishes. He could now walk a bit but continued to use the wheelchair to increase his mobility and to give the two girls something to do. "Let's go to the shop and build something."

"What do you want to build this time? Last week we tried our hand at a dog house and what we ended up with was something too heavy to move, too big to go through the door, and too ugly for any discriminating dog to call home. We had to dismantle it so we'd have enough wood to build something else."

"This time we're going to learn the art of measurement. And when we have that squared away we can build something pleasant to look at."

"Okay. I've heard that Spencer's building a racer for the Soap Box Derby. Could we build one of those so I could race with him? The grand prize is four years paid tuition at any state university."

"That sounds great. But before we get started, we ought to see how Spencer is coming along."

"It's all hush-hush, Edwin. Spencer is not letting anyone see his project. He thinks other people will use his ideas and if they add one improvement to his basic design he will be at a disadvantage."

"Surely he wouldn't believe an old man in a wheelchair and two girls could give him any competition."

"You're right. Let's go check it out. Issie, get Edwin's Panama."

While Issie pushed, Laurie walked beside Edwin. "Have you ever driven a soap box derby racer?"

"No. I don't think they had races like that when I was your age. But then again, we're pretty much in the sticks out here. A lot of things happen in those big towns back east that never seem to make it to rural Arkansas. How many races will Spencer have to win?"

"He doesn't know for sure. He read about last year's race at the library and is worried he might not get to race at all. The closest town holding a local race is Kansas City. He'd have to beat everyone there before he'd be able to go to Derby Downs in Akron, Ohio. There they get all the local race winners from across the United States and a few from other countries that qualified in preliminary races at the Downs and match them up—three cars to a heat. You have to keep winning because the first heat that you don't cross the finish line first sends you packing.

"Spencer worked it out. He said that if they started with a hundred and fifty boys that would mean they would have fifty races with three boys racing in each. Those fifty winners would square off against each other in seventeen races. Then those seventeen race winners would be pitted against each other in six races, then two, and then one race between the two fastest cars in the area. So Spencer has decided that he has to win five races to get to go to the Downs. There he'll have to win another five, or possibly six, races and he'll come home a hero with a college degree in his future. I'm excited for him."

When the sidewalk ran out Issie asked, "Laurie, are you sure he lives way out here?"

"Yeah, a family living on a farm adopted he and Millie. It's just another block or so. I think they're still considered as living in Dancing Deer—just at the far edge."

"Issie, stop for a minute and let me walk. If I used the wheelchair handles to hold onto I could use it as a walker."

"Mr. Stanky, you're no problem to push. It's just so hot. When we get there what're we going to do if he's not home?"

Laurie said, "He'll be there. But we should have called first."

In a few more minutes Laurie said, "Here let me push for a while. Their house is at the top of the hill."

"Whew. It's a good thing because when the sidewalk ran out, and we had to use the road I was afraid we'd be run over. It's a miracle there hasn't been any traffic."

"Edwin, do you think we could have stopped at Ava's Dresses and picked up your car? I could steer while you pushed down on the accelerator—or the brake—with your foot."

"And if we met traffic?"

"I could keep it in our lane?"

"Young lady, Gladys would have to bail us out of the pokey. Can you imagine the headlines? 'Local Girl takes Geezer on Joy Ride.'"

All three were still laughing when they made it to Spencer's front door. Gus and May Poindexter had adopted Millie and Spencer. It was Mrs. Poindexter who escorted the trio to the barn where Spencer was at a table sketching something on a large tablet with Gus sitting on a nearby stool offering his opinion.

"I'm only saying that you got to see over the steering wheel somehow." Gus was pointing at the paper.

"Yoo-hoo, boys. We got company." May announced their presence.

"Hello, Gus . . . and Spencer. We've come by to see if there is any truth to the rumor that Barney Oldfield has come back from the dead and is planning on entering some down-hill race."

"Come in, Edwin. This boy has a lotta spunk. He's putting together a plan to get his education paid. All he has to do is build a contraption that can go faster than any other similar contraption built by any other similar boy in the entire United States. He feels so strongly in his ability to do so that he's talked May out of her egg money to buy his parts and me into letting him tear down part of the barn for the wood. And the boy won't let me help—not that I want to. Well, yes I do."

"Gus, that doesn't seem fair."

"That's what I told him, but he showed me in the rule book that he could only take advice from someone else. He has to build the contraption himself. So, I'm giving plenty of advice."

"Spencer, I've built a few things in my day. If you and Gus come on a problem you can't resolve, I'd like to give you my opinion and loan you my tools. Does it say in the rule book you have to use your own tools?"

"No. A couple of saws would be good. Everything we have is dull and rusty."

"You got it. What about hinges, nails, screws . . . things like that?"

"I have to supply everything that doesn't come with the wheels and axles kit."

"I think Laurie is planning on building one. You got any suggestions she could use to get started."

"Ha ha. Laurie? Miss Stansberry, are you not aware girls are banned from competing?"

"What?"

"That's right. I read it in the rule book."

"Well, that's not fair. I'm going to ask Mr. Jellico if he'll write a letter. We need to get that rule changed."

May came through the barn door carrying a pitcher followed by Millie with a stack of glasses. "Can I interest anyone in a glass of iced tea?"

Laurie held out a shovel to Edwin. Slowly Edwin stood from his wheelchair and, gripping the shovel handle with both hands to steady his walk, made his way around the table. Looking at Spencer's drawings, Edwin said, "Since there is no way Laurie and I can be your competition do you mind showing us what you have planned for this speeding machine?"

CHAPTER 15 – THE WIND ARRIVES

September, 1946

A large truck arrived at Andy Muldoon's house. Two men got out with one starting to unlatch the rear door while the driver walked to the house with a clipboard holding down several papers needing to be signed.

Rex said he could sign for his father, or the man could drive by the bank on the way out of town if he needed to get an official signature. The man mulled it over in his head and said he'd decide after he saw the boy's effort at forging his father's name. He then asked where the young man wanted the delivery placed.

"In the kitchen."

"Son, the crate won't fit through the doorway. How about the garage."

"Okay. I'll get the key."

Twenty minutes later the men had left, and Rex was sitting cross-legged on a sizable wooden box swinging a hammer at the end of a crowbar.

"This is *The Wind*—I just know it. Mr. Wind are you in there?"

A piece of two-by-four came loose at one end, and Rex stood pulling the board up with him. He heard a screeching sound as the nails holding down the other end bended and slid out of a stubborn cross-member. Rex threw the wooden strip to the floor.

After thirty minutes, Rex had to take a break. The treasure chest was not willing to give up its cargo easily, and Rex's arm was quivering from swinging the heavy framing hammer. After a short break, Rex was back at it, and twenty minutes later *The Wind* made its appearance. It was wrapped in a soft cotton moving quilt. When Rex pulled back its cover, he let out a soft whistle.

"I have it. *The Wind* is here. I have *The Wind* and its all mine." Rex pulled it out of the opened crate and sat on the floor looking at it. "I can't believe it—*The Wind*. Your twin brother won the derby by completely demolishing the competition. It never lost a race. No other racer even came close."

Rex walked over to his new prize and carefully crawled into the seat. He grabbed the steering wheel and leaned forward. His imagination ran wild. He saw himself screaming down the track with a scarf around his head fluttering behind like a cape. People cheering in the stands. The other racers left in his dust. A radio announcer calling out the racer's positions at the quarter, the half, and the three-quarter marks.

"*The Wind* in the lead at the quarter mark by two lengths with the other cars falling farther behind. At the half, it's *The Wind* by five lengths. Let me see that stop watch. Ladies and Gentlemen, *The Wind* is on a torrid pace. If he keeps this up he will set a new world record. At the three-quarter mark, it's *The Wind* in the lead by half a mile. Wait a minute, is that smoke coming from the wheels? And *The Wind* wins with his competition just now coming into view."

At a little after five Rex's father pulled into the driveway. Rex was still sitting in the roadster. "What do you think? Is that not a fine gift?"

"Dad, when will I get to race it?

"Next summer."

"Not before then?"

"No. Besides we have to make some alterations. The new rules say you have to use wheels and axles purchased from the Derby authorities, and the seat has to be removable for inspection. It has to have a brake. And we have to see how far the nose sticks out in front of the tires—that distance is now limited. They are constantly changing the rules to keep people from cheating."

"Dad, why would someone want to cheat at a Soap Box Derby race?"

"A four-year college scholarship is quite an incentive. Some people don't believe in fair play, it's the winning that matters and are willing to do whatever it takes. Come on inside. Nelda called to say she wouldn't be able to cook our supper tonight. So you're going to have to put up with whatever I can slap together."

CHAPTER 16 – THE CALHOUN CONSTRUCTION COMPANY

Early October, 1946

Rupert Calhoun watched his employees work. They had spent the last three weeks erecting bleachers for the soapbox derby track being constructed in Skunk Hollow. Another contractor had already laid the asphalt and rolled smooth a thousand-foot track thirty feet wide. They then striped three 10-foot lanes. The track was extended another three hundred feet, with no stripes, past the finish line. The track ended in a wide circle to give the racers plenty of room to slow down and come to a complete stop. A gravel road had been graded on the north side of the tracks from the stopping area back to the finish line so that a pickup truck dragging a flatbed trailer could haul the racers back for additional heats.

Above the starting area were pits where minor adjustments could be made to the racers before competing and a staging area where nine cars lined up three deep and three abreast awaiting their turn to enter the starting gates. A few feet from the hullabaloo of the starting area was a gravel pad where a local mechanic would be available should any racer's safety issue need to be resolved.

Before the bleachers had been started, Rupert's crew had installed metal posts sticking three feet above the ground, twenty feet apart, and in two rows six feet left and right of the track. From these posts would be strung two strands of a narrow gauge steel cable to keep onlookers from wandering onto the track or interfering with the race in some manner. Along the way three platforms had been built where judges, wearing African safari hats, could watch the race and make sure the rules were abided by. In addition, there would be two officials at the start and three at the finish line.

The Calhoun Construction Company had been contracted to install the posts and cable and to build the bleachers, and judges' platforms. The starting gates were being constructed by a local outfit based in

Skunk Hollow. When this new carpentry company had contacted the Calhoun Construction Company to purchase wood, Claude had said all of their wood was needed for other on-going projects and gave them names of two other suppliers.

"Just a minute. The sawmill in Moccasin Gap said they had contracted with you for the purchase of their entire output, and now you're telling me you're using everything they can produce?"

"That's exactly what I'm saying."

"Well, those other sawmills you mentioned will charge a hefty delivery fee, and we had to make our bid so low that we don't have any excess. It'll take all our profit to get the material."

"You should have thought of that before you made the low bid."

"See here, Calhoun. You can't monopolize the market. I'll have to let the authorities know."

"Please do. From now on you'll have to contact us through our legal council—Mr. Michael Jellico." Claude's call abruptly ended as the person he was talking to slammed down the telephone.

The Calhoun Construction Company was given blueprints for construction of five movable bleachers each holding 150 people and placed along the track on the southern side. They were also supplied a hand drawing giving the dimensions for the judge's platforms. During the construction, an official had periodically inspected their work to make sure they had built to the specifications required.

Rupert helped Spencer string the cable through the metal posts. "I think we're going to meet our deadline with a day or two to spare. How are you coming with your racer, Spence?"

"It's not finished yet. I'm sure glad you had time to show me how to bend wood. That was a lot faster than me piecing together small chunks I had cut at angles."

"Glad to help. Bending wood is easy if the wood is saturated with water and you bend it in small increments over a period of time. So how much more you got to do?"

"Attach the windshield and seat, hook up the brake, and paint."

"The hardest part of that will be the painting. Put on a primer first and then several thin coats of paint with a light sanding between coats. Let each coat dry before sanding and before the last coat of paint use a cotton cloth instead of sand paper. What color are you going with?"

"I'm not sure but British Racing Green comes to mind."

"Whoa. Just think how smart you'll be looking in saddle tan leathers and helmet."

"Mr. Calhoun, I would rather win in my underwear than look good and not win."

"Spence, you are a driven boy. With your eye on the ball, everything you do is geared to winning this race. And I hope you do, but you've got to realize that winning is not everything. You'll use the things you learn here for the rest of your life. You'll learn how to set goals, how to apportion your time and resources, how to develop your skills, how to compete given the rules you have to comply with, and how to win or lose gracefully.

"Have you heard that on Saturday, at the racetrack's grand opening festivities, there will be a trial run by a racer already completed. Some kid recently moved into Skunk Hollow, and he has a racer. He named it *The Wind*. You got a name for yours?"

"Not yet. Will you be going to Skunk Hollow Saturday?"

"I surely will—me and the missus."

"And taking the truck?"

"Probably. You need a lift?"

"Yes, sir. I want to see my competition."

Three men sat in a diner in downtown Skunk Hollow. One was reading the local paper, *The Skunk Hollow Fever*. A second was reading a competing paper from Dancing Deer, a neighboring town.

"So Fred, what do you think?"

"Ssh. Let's keep it low. Everyone in here is trying to listen in on our conversation. But I think we need to find some other location. This town doesn't have but two restaurants and neither one is what I'd call . . . um," the man put a hand over his mouth, "decent."

"I disagree. They have a superior track and seating for seven hundred and fifty spectators. And there is a new French restaurant soon to be open for business."

"I don't know. The housing is almost non-existent. There are two run-down hotels on the highway to Russellville and a newly renovated park with bathroom facilities. I do have to admit they have a beautiful location for the park. They even have electrical outlets in each camping space, but how many racing fans will want to rough it by camping out?

The third man spoke for the first time. "We shouldn't be hasty in making our decision. We need a local race in Arkansas, and Little Rock says their racetrack won't be ready by next summer. They say they have to get a bond issue passed so the city will have the necessary funds. I really think they have too many hoops to jump through.

"If we could get Skunk Hollow to invest in better accommodations it might work—at least until Little Rock gets its act together. Why don't we go into this with open eyes and hope that Skunk Hollow can pull it together."

"You're right John. Let's keep everything to ourselves and tell Mayor Thompkins the things his town will have to come up with to stay in the running. But we'll hold off on saying anything until we're about to leave town."

CHAPTER 17 – THE CIRCUS
October 12, 1946

On Friday October 11, 1946 Sydney Rene walked into Andy Muldoon's office carrying an envelope.

"Andy, have you tried the new restaurant?"

"Not yet."

"I had some misgivings at first, but I have to admit, the food was wonderful. And the service extraordinary. I didn't know we had people in Skunk Hollow capable of providing that level of service. I've heard she's been training her staff for months."

"I'm sorry, she?"

"Yes. The owner is—was—a friend of mine. Oh and I have the tickets our kids won at Russell's birthday party."

"Russell's birthday party?"

"Have you forgotten? Rex and Lydia won the three-legged race and their prize was two tickets on the front row for the circus." She held out the envelope.

"Yes. I remember. And a Major won two tickets for the tow sack race."

"Correct."

Andy Muldoon opened the envelope. "Sydney, there's only one ticket in here."

Correct again. I've already given Lydia hers. Can you have Rex there by six tomorrow evening? I thought they might like to walk down the midway or to get cotton candy before being seated at seven."

"Is this a date?"

"Good heavens no. I merely had the seats purchased together when I thought the winners would all be boys, and they could sit together as a group. That way they would have someone they knew to talk with.

"My ex-husband and I will be seated a few rows up to make sure the kids are safe."

"Good, because I don't have a ticket. I have a mountain of work I'll be tackling at the kitchen table."

"Andy, you need to get out more. Check out the new restaurant. All work and no play makes Jack a dull boy."

"I'm about as dull as they get."

"There was once a woman who didn't think you were all that dull."

"She was taken off her guard and didn't come to realize the truth of the matter until a short time later, when it was too late."

"How long were you married?"

"Three years. She looks back on that as three years of her life stolen and leaving her with impaired appeal. So, what is this about you and your ex-husband. Are you getting back together?"

"Good heavens no. I would give it another shot, but he thinks he's escaped the clutches of his worst nightmare. I've always been an opinionated woman—hard to dance with as well. I have to lead."

The next afternoon Andy dropped off his son and returned home to a pile of papers needing immediate care. Rex liked the circus. Someone was always trying to pull something over on him and he thought it hilarious to watch a huckster make an effort to lure him into a financial transaction that would leave the huckster with his money and him with some toy that didn't work, was rusted underneath a hand painted cover, or wasn't the item offered anyway. Rex stopped at a wagon selling hotdogs and bought two.

"Are one of those for me?"

"Uh . . no. Hello, Lydia."

"Well, buy me one with sauerkraut. And a beverage."

"Hmm."

Two boys walked up, pushed Lydia out of their way, and started to order. Rex bumped into the biggest one, spilling his beverage on the boy's pants.

"Oh. Sorry about that. Here hold this." Rex handed his hotdogs to the second boy and kneed the first boy, the one with wet pants. From the boy now holding his hotdogs, Rex took the dollar the boy had been offering the vendor. Rex said, "Thanks. I'll need this to replace my drink." Rex then stepped hard on the foot of the boy with the wet pants and shoved him in the chest. With his foot penned, the boy lost his balance and fell into the wagon. Rex took back his two hotdogs and said, "Help your friend up then get out of my way. Next time remember to let girls go first." Rex turned to the vendor and ordered another drink for himself and the two items asked for by Lydia. When he turned back to Lydia, the two boys were gone.

"Whew. That happened fast. I thought you were clumsy at first."

"Me, clumsy? Never. I just have big hands and feet. And an attitude."

"Yes. Just like my mother. Except she's more devious, and you're more physical. Still, I don't believe in intentionally hurting someone. At some point, you have to start growing up."

"Hmm."

Rex and Lydia ate their hotdogs as they walked to the big tent in the center of things. After handing over their tickets and being escorted to the front row Lydia said, "Do you want me to exchange my ticket for one of Major's?"

"No, you're good."

The rest of the evening Rex and Lydia were thoroughly entertained. Clowns filled the arena between acts. They threw confetti into the stands, wore outlandish clothing with massive shoes and funny hats, and played stupid tricks on each other. The first act was of a man throwing knives at a woman standing in front of a wooden sign. Every knife landed close to her body, piercing the wood with a loud twang. The second act was of some horses running around in a large circle with several women jumping from one to another. One woman even stood up with her feet firmly planted on the backs of two horses. Then there was a man who walked on a wire, one man and two women swinging on a trapeze, and a very brave man who made three lions perform tricks on upturned barrels.

At the end of the performance, the crowd whooped it up as they stood, clapped, and cheered to show their appreciation.

Lydia said, "That was amazing. I especially liked the horses."

"Yeah. But, for me, I liked the scary parts and those lions."

CHAPTER 18 – SACRE BLEU CAFE

October, 1946

Andre was worried. A new restaurant had opened in Skunk Hollow to raving reviews. Some of his patrons had bragged that the food and service they received when trying the new venue compared favorably to a dining experience at his Ritz Grand Hotel and Ballroom Bistro. Andre needed to check things out for himself.

As soon as the noon rush had died down Andre washed his hands, removed his chef's hat and apron, ran a comb through his hair, twirled the ends of his mustache, and told his employees to mind the store. On his way out, he asked Gerald to join him. Gerald had a car.

On the drive to Skunk Hollow, Andre told Gerald they needed to keep a low profile. It was probably not necessary to inform anybody who they were, where they were from, and for what purpose they were partaking of their competitor's delicacies. "Gerald, I thought you would enjoy a short adventure and I'll need a second opinion."

"Sure boss. Are you paying? I don't have any money."

"Of course. Order anything you like. Anything other than what I'm ordering. And I'll want a bite of each item."

"Dessert as well?"

"Especially dessert."

"Man! What a treat."

When the duo arrived in Skunk Hollow, they drove down main street amazed at the number of new businesses and pedestrians. Gerald pulled into a parking space fifty yards from where the new restaurant was spilling out its clientele onto wrought iron tables and chairs on the sidewalk. The parking spaces in front of the restaurant had been blocked off with the sidewalk being extended, and a pedestrian walkway routed around a low brick wall. Ten tables now adorned the sidewalk—each with occupants eating, placing their orders, waiting on their orders, or relaxing with cups of espresso while they put off the trip back to work.

Waiters came through wide openings in the front of the building carrying circular trays of food above their heads. Inside the building were more tables.

"Boss, they have a lot of customers."

"Yes, they do. Let's go inside to see if it is just an opening frenzy for a new restaurant or if their patronage is deserved."

A very attractive woman with flashing black eyes greeted them at a small podium. "Will there be two for lunch?"

"Oui, Mademoiselle."

"Please follow me. There are no tables available outside, and we have three parties waiting, but we have a lovely table inside I can seat you at right now."

"Charming."

The woman handed Andre and Gerald tall menus full of pictures showing what was available. "A waiter will be by in a moment to take your orders and to bring you water."

"Please, Mademoiselle. Are all of these items available for lunch?"

"Yes. Lunch is a slightly smaller serving-size and the lesser of the two prices."

"Fantastic. Are you always this busy?"

"No, Monsieur. In the evenings, it is suggested you make reservations."

Andre and Gerald were mightily impressed—Andre more so with the delectable creature with the flashing eyes.

On the ride back to Dancing Deer, Andre was in a quiet, introspective mood. Gerald thought he was depressed because the new restaurant was so pleasurable and backed off to give Andre time to get his act together.

The next day Andre called to say he wasn't feeling well and didn't want to cook anyway. When asked if he was sick, Andre had to admit that he was not. It was just a mental condition, and he should be better the next day.

The second day back Gerald came in at his regular time and Andre was already there reworking his menus. Several of his cookbooks littered the work area.

"Gerald, do you know how the Catholic church responded to the protestant movement started by Martin Luther?"

"No."

"They reformed. They came back stronger than ever with a clearer message, a more fervent effort to stay true to their charge of bringing the word to the masses, and a cleansing of the waste and poor practices.

"Is that what you're doing—reforming the Bistro?"

"I've been wondering what that woman would think of my restaurant if she came in here like we went into hers."

"Was that tall woman at the maitre d's station the owner?"

"I think so. And I have to say I thought she was as remarkable as her place of business."

"Andre, you've got stars in your eyes."

CHAPTER 19 – BEHOLD, THE WIND

Late October, 1946

On a warm Saturday in late October of 1946 the citizens of Skunk Hollow assembled in their city park beside their new soap box racetrack to celebrate its completion and grand opening. Even a hundred or more people from Dancing Deer had come bringing a wagon holding ripe watermelons, buckets of home-made ice cream, and lawn chairs. They quickly added their food from the wagon to long tables already laden with food supplied by fellow citizens from Skunk Hollow.

In front of the starting gates, a small raised platform on wheels was positioned with a podium and a microphone. Red, white, and blue bunting festooned all stationery posts. Tied together balloons completely covered a long curved sign hanging high above. And the flag of the United States flew alongside the Arkansas state flag. A tuba band got everyone's attention with an enthusiastic rendering of *America, The Beautiful*. Then a prayer was given, and everyone was asked to stand while the tuba band played the *Star Spangled Banner*.

The mayor of skunk Hollow walked across a portable platform to the microphone. He thumped it one time to make sure it was turned on and said, "I'm Asa Thompkins, the mayor of Skunk Hollow, and I want to extend a hearty Skunk Hollow welcome to everyone able to come celebrate the grand opening of our new racetrack dedicated to the Soap Box Derby Racers.

"It's been built to the specifications supplied us by the All American Soap Box Derby Association. We are happy to have officials from that Association here today. They have been here for a while checking out our friendly faces, the amiable hospitality, and the beautiful town we call home. Skunk Hollow is being considered by their Association to be an integral part of the annual Soap Box Derby extravaganza. If selected we will host a local race here on an annual basis with the winner receiving an all expense paid trip to Derby Downs in Akron, Ohio along with a few other items like this new Schwinn bicycle.

"At Akron's Derby Downs our winner will compete against more than one hundred local race winners from across the United States in an effort to be crowned the winner of the All American Soap Box Derby."

Here the mayor had to pause while the loud clapping and the hip-hip-hooraying took over. A few moments later he introduced the visiting officials and continued with, "So, fellow citizens and racing enthusiasts, let these fine gentlemen know how much we appreciate being afforded this opportunity. And now it is my extreme pleasure to officially open . . ." The mayor pointed to a young man on his right and another on his left who promptly cut the ropes holding back helium filled balloons. When they were let loose, they sailed high in the air exposing a colorful display board with the racetrack name—"The Soap Box Derby Grand Prix of Skunk Hollow."

"Now if everyone will clear the track by getting behind the cable, and I can get someone to move this platform, we will see our own Rex Muldoon display his racer. And if everyone agrees, we'll coerce him into being the first participant to run the course. Are you all with me on this?"

There was enthusiastic yelling from all sides as Rex walked to a sofa covered by a nondescript quilted covering. Someone yanked off the covering to display a sleeping mass of high energy skinned in a sleek, vibrant blue trimmed in navy. Amid the whistling, the begging, and the pleading Rex put on his goggles and helmet then crawled into *The Wind*. His father pushed him to the starting gate.

Rex waited and then waited a little longer until the crowd hushed to see just how fast this thing could go. When he was ready Rex grabbed the steering wheel and leaned forward. The starter lowered a checkered flag and a flap holding back *The Wind* fell to the ground with *The Wind* jumping out of the gate.

The Wind was going fast from the moment it leaped over the starting flap. In fact, it was scaring Rex. He reached one hand under his goggles to wipe the sweat from his brow or maybe it was a tear in the corner of his eye. With only one hand on the steering wheel *The Wind* did a wobble with Rex overcorrecting. One more wobble and Rex gained control just before *The Wind* spun out. From there to the finish line Rex held a death grip on the steering wheel and both eyes on the road. When he got past the finish line, he lowered the brake and pushed down with his foot. The brake made contact with the asphalt and was held down by the foot of a nervous driver trying to finish his first race. *The Wind* slowed and then stopped. Rex was glad his first run was over. He slowly crawled out taking off his helmet and goggles.

Lydia ran up saying, "Rex, that was wonderful. But it looked like the car had a mind of its own, and you were just hanging on. How do you feel? You look a bit woozy."

"Yeah, riding *The Wind* is like being strapped to a tornado."

Rupert looked at Spencer. "Spence, I hope your racer is fast because the competition is tough."

"I know. I'm starting over tomorrow."

CHAPTER 20 – THE INSPECTION
Late October, 1946

Three men were making their way to the finish line as fast as they could. "Lionel, wait up. My legs aren't as long as yours, and I'm carrying eighty more pounds. Besides, John is even farther back than me."

Over his shoulder, the man in the lead said rather loudly, "Fred, I got to get there before the boy has a chance to hide whatever he's done to make his racer so blamed fast. You and John get there when you can." And with that the man in the lead changed gears and speeded up.

When Fred and John arrived Lionel had everyone moved away from the racer, and he had pulled out the seat to inspect the transmission. John hoisted the front end off the ground, and Fred positioned a lawn chair under its nose so that the front two wheels spun freely. After John gently lowered the chassis onto the lawn chair, he got down on the ground and started inspecting the under-carriage. Fred spun both front wheels then checked the bearings to make sure Rex Muldoon had used Derby authorized parts. In a few minutes, all three were huddled in a small ring.

Lionel said, "I couldn't find one thing wrong. However, there also were no marks showing where the boy's wrench slipped, or indentations showing a patch or a work-around. This thing looks like it was made on the Ferrari production line by skilled craftsmen."

"Same thing I found. He used authorized parts with serial numbers showing they had been recently purchased. There were no grease smears, no wear marks where two items had rubbed against one another. John what did you find?"

"You'll not believe what I found. It appears each nut was tightened with a torque wrench giving the exact pressure necessary to keep the nut from vibrating loose and not over tight so as to press the shoulder washer into the wood. I'm impressed . . . and a little worried."

"Yeah, how could a twelve-year-old boy have built it to this standard of craftsmanship?"

Lionel said, "Let's go talk to him . . . and his father."

"I agree but we need to be discreet. Let's not let them know what our misgivings are. Let's not let them know what we suspect so they'll have time to formulate an excuse or make changes to the racer in an effort to assuage our concern," said Fred.

That evening the three judges met with Rex Muldoon and his father.

"Gentlemen, may I offer anyone iced tea?" Andy Muldoon was worried his son would not be able to keep his wits. He thought if they would just let me answer their questions I could make them believe Rex had actually built the racer himself and everything would be okay.

"No, thank you Mr. Muldoon. We have to be on our way as soon as we can. We've been here far too long as it is. We have another place to be tomorrow with a long drive to get there. We just want to talk with your son about the production of *The Wind*—that is what he named it, didn't he?"

Rex was standing in the doorway with a worried look on his face.

"Yeah, his cousin won the derby when Rex was a young boy. And a few years ago I took Rex to your Hall of Fame in Akron. His cousin's racer is on display with pictures of him accepting the trophy and of him crossing the finish line. Rex was so envious that he's dreamed about accomplishing the same feat. His cousin's car was named *The Wind*, so Rex built his racer to look like the one on display and used the same name.

All three men turned to look at Rex, who had entered the room and sat down beside his dad.

Lionel said, "So Rex, have you ever raced before?"

"No."

"Has your racer ever raced before?"

"No."

"Where is your cousin—the one who won the derby in his version of *The Wind*?"

"In Philadelphia. He goes to the University of Pennsylvania."

"Do you get to see him often?"

"No."

"When was the last time you saw him?"

"Last year at our family reunion. I played flag football with him while our parents were barbecuing."

"So, did you get to spend much time with him?"

"No. He's ten years older than me and has a girlfriend. He didn't say much of anything to me."

Fred got up from his chair and walked around the sofa thinking. He had his arm bent across his chest and held his chin in his hand. He said, "How did you develop your carpentry skills."

"Dad and I have converted our garage into a workshop. We used to build things together but now, with his new job at the bank, he doesn't have much time, so I tinker around on my own."

"Did your dad help you build your racer?"

"No."

"Did anyone help you build your racer?"

"No."

"Have you built any other items we could look at?"

"I have a couple of bird feeders."

"And you developed your skill to build a derby racer by slapping together a bird feeder."

"I was also a Boy Scout and a Cub Scout before that. I had projects that I built while belonging to those organizations. And once I made a box in vacation bible school."

"A box?"

"Yeah. One no one could open."

"Why couldn't they open it?"

"It had a circular lock that wouldn't unlock unless you spun it around making three weights overcome a weak spring to slide out of their slots by centrifugal force."

"Wonderful. Could we see this box no one could open?"

"No. It was auctioned off to pay for summer camp. My box sold for the most money of any item auctioned."

"How about the bird feeders?"

"Yeah, they're in the back yard."

All three men stood and followed the boy and his father into the back yard.

"Being a single father I've had to come up with activities to keep the boy from getting bored or into trouble. During the week, I don't have much time to spend with him, so I make up for it on the weekends."

Lionel said, "Well, he did a remarkable job with the racer."

Fred said, "So, what is so remarkable about these bird feeders."

"Nothing really. We don't have many trees so I put one on top of a metal flagpole I had Dad cement into the ground and this other I hung from a branch of a sweet gum tree."

"So?"

"So, the one on the pole worked perfectly except I had to stand on top of our car to add feed to it once a week. The other kept getting robbed by squirrels, so I added obstacles for them to overcome to get to the feed."

"And did that work?"

"No. Those squirrels are smart. They would work and work, finally figuring a way to the feed, and I'd have to add another problem for them to solve. Right now there is only one squirrel smart enough to get to the feed, so I named her Baba Yaga."

"A Russian Witch?"

"Yep. Got the name from a book in the library."

"Okay. Tell us how your obstacles work."

"First I had to put a wooden roof above the bird feeder to keep the squirrels from simply jumping down from the tree branch the feeder was hanging from. Then I had to move it to a branch farther away from the trunk of the tree because after hanging the roof they started jumping straight from the tree. That worked for a while until they went back to jumping onto the roof, sliding down, and then swinging to the feeder. By then it had become fun, so I replaced the roof with a metal cone much bigger so that the bottom extended farther away from the feeder. I also placed a wire from the tree trunk to the feeder. When they figured out how to walk the wire, I greased it, and they slid off until one of them figured out how to hang upside down and pull along with its front feet. That's when I cut the wire and fashioned a fan between the two wire halves. One of the two wires I left attached to the tree trunk and stretched to the top of the fan shroud. The second wire I stretched from the bottom of the fan shroud to the feeder. I then pulled the wire taut. I had to add more wiring to keep the fan perpendicular to the ground. When I finished, and the wind blew, the blades rotated. A squirrel could climb upside down along the wire, and jump aboard the fan blade at the top taking a ride until it stopped at the bottom of its arc. At the bottom, she stepped through the shroud to the wire on the other side and continued along it to the feeder. Only one squirrel could do it, so that's when I named her and now keep her in feed."

"Marvelous. That's all the questions I have. Fred do you have anymore?"

"No."

"John, how about you?"

"No. But I want to check the track's gradient before we leave."

"Okay, we better head there right now. Thank you, Mr. Muldoon and you, Rex for meeting with us. And good luck racing *The Wind*."

In their car John said, "Either of you believe the boy built that racer?"

"Not for one minute. Did anyone notice the size of his hands? There is no way he could counter-sink a finishing nail and not leave marks on the wood."

"He could have covered it over with wood putty before sanding and painting."

"I thought of that but didn't see any putty or paint among his supplies."

"Or torque wrench or leather shears, scissors, needles, or waxed thread. I mean those seats looked like they were made by an Italian craftsman cobbling expensive gloves or shoes."

"What should we do?"

"I think we should do a little research on the boy's cousin and the original *Wind*."

CHAPTER 21 – AN AGREEMENT

Early November, 1946

"Jesse, you received a letter from the Skunk Hollow Downtown Revitalization Committee. I put it on your desk."

Jesse stepped out of the break room with a fresh cup of coffee. "Thank you, Midge. What do you think it's about?"

"Probably to get you to run their advertisement asking businesses to relocate to a new and vibrant Skunk Hollow."

"I did that once and won't do it again." Jesse sat at his desk looking at an envelope with a black and white cat sporting a fluffy tail adorning the top left corner. A few minutes later Jesse was asking if Jack had returned with the delivery truck.

"I was headed in to talk to you. All of the racks were chained shut. I couldn't leave the first paper in Skunk Hollow. Even the restaurants said they didn't want any. What's going on, Jesse?"

"I don't know. We'll go pick up the racks and see what happens."

The *Marsden County Meteor* delivery truck and two distraught occupants cruised Skunk Hollow's Main Street looking for the offices of the Skunk Hollow Downtown Revitalization Committee. Jesse noticed several new retail stores, a new restaurant with people eating out-front on the sidewalk around small tables, and a new office building. The marquee outside the office building said it was the Kilburn Building and listed two businesses: the *Skunk Hollow Fever* newspaper with the second being the one they were trying to find.

Jesse noticed that, besides having new businesses, there were more shoppers than he had expected. There were also more automobiles. "It looks like Skunk Hollow is thriving."

"Yeah. Everybody here is excited about this new race the boys are going to have next summer. It was the jolt they needed to get off their cans and do something. Mr. Bell, why is the race going to be staged in Skunk Hollow and not in Dancing Deer?"

"Because Jack, they have new members on their city council. The mayor said no one was working with him, and the voters agreed. Now the mayor—Asa Thompkins—has a whole new group of helpers, and they're trying their best to make the city think their mandate meant something."

"And Dancing Deer is just going to watch from the sidelines?"

"No Jack, Dancing Deer is not falling behind while Skunk Hollow forges ahead. Everyone wins in situations like this. Competition is good for us and everyone living in this part of Northern Arkansas.

"Jack, if you were watching a basketball game between Skunk Hollow and some team from Georgia or Nebraska which one would you be rooting for?"

"Uh . . . my favorite teams, in any sport, are Dancing Deer and whoever is playing Skunk Hollow."

"I forgot who I was talking to. Try and stay out of trouble for a few minutes while I speak with the people who sent me that nasty note."

"You got it, boss. I'll mosey around a bit and meet you at the new restaurant in thirty minutes."

Jesse was humming a tune when he went in and mumbling under his breath when he came out. "They want me to pick up my racks. Say there is no demand for any paper other than their own *Fever*. Someone has pushed for a new ordinance asking businesses to buy local. Well, this reeks of censorship." Jesse paused in front of the door to the *Skunk Hollow Fever* then went in.

"May I help you?"

"I need to speak with the owner . . . the uh, editor."

"Mr. Kilburn is taking pictures of the *Aurora Borealis* in Yellow Knife, but Patricia Kilburn, his daughter and our editor, is here. Have a seat, and I'll see if she can see you. May I have your name?"

"I'm Jesse Bell."

"From the *Meteor*?" Jesse nodded. "I'll be right back."

In a few minutes, three men wearing suits and carrying briefcases walked down the hall to the reception area and through the front door into the foyer of the Kilburn Building. On their heels came an attractive woman holding out her hand.

"Good morning, Mr. Bell. My name is Patricia Kilburn. I feel like I already know you. I've been reading your editorials and your responses to the 'Letters to the Editor' since I was a child."

"You're probably thinking of my father. The *Meteor* was his paper until a few years ago."

"I see. Well, what can I do for you, sir?"

"Do you sell many papers in Dancing Deer?"

"No, not many."

"Would you take offence if the authorities in Dancing Deer said you couldn't sell your papers in their town?"

"Probably. Is that what the Revitalization Committee told you?"

"Yes."

"I had nothing to do with any announcement like that. You have the right to sell your papers anywhere you please—and I, as well. We can't make anyone read our literary efforts—or not read them. Its up to each person to make that decision. What would you like for me to do?"

"Nothing. The people here can get their news from your paper. I wasn't selling many papers and not much advertising either so I'll enhance my bottom line by cutting a loss leader. But, while I'm here, we should talk a little about the Soap Box Derby."

"Skunk Hollow is pretty excited about that possibility. Those three men who just left are the officials sent here to assess our ability to hold the race and for my paper to be its sponsor."

"Is that expensive?"

"Yeah. It's going to eat up my entire discretionary budget. I hadn't planned on it and didn't budget for it so now everything else is on hold while I try and fulfill the Derby's demands."

"Like readership, exposure, and ponying up for the purse?"

"Precisely."

"Would you care to share? If I added my subscriber tally and area of coverage to yours, we would probably meet the first two conditions. And if we were to hyphenate the name of our papers and split the costs for sending the race winner to Ohio your budget would not be ruined."

"And I have to pay a portion of the prizes given out to the eventual winners in Akron."

"To be split as well."

"Let me think about it. Can I reach you at your paper's office?"

"Yeah."

The rest of the day Jesse thought about the logistics of sponsoring the All American Soap Box Derby Race in Akron, Ohio with another paper. Jack thought Jesse was upset with him for some reason so didn't question Jesse when he noticed his boss had a far-away look in his eyes. During their lunch and on the drive back Jesse was quiet, and Jack was nervous.

Entering the *Meteor*'s office Jesse said, "Midge, send someone to Skunk Hollow to take pictures of their new racetrack and the new businesses in town. Send someone with him to interview a few people. I want the gist of what the word is on the street."

CHAPTER 22 – THE APPLICATION

Early November, 1946

"Mr. Bell, Gus said you wanted to talk to me."

"How are you doing, Spence? That was some performance that Skunk Hollow kid gave with his racer. And I was impressed with its fit and finish. It looked like professionals made it. And could it fly! I wanted to check to see if you were still resolved to building yours and racing *The Wind?*"

"Mr. Bell, all of the orphans have had to deal with setbacks. The only way we could come to grips with our situation was to buckle down and persevere. *The Wind* is only another obstacle I have to overcome."

Jesse was impressed with Spencer's determined attitude. If there was anyone capable of building a car good enough to best *The Wind,* Spencer was the one. "Okay, the *Marsden County Meteor* is teaming up with the *Skunk Hollow Fever* to sponsor next year's local race in Skunk Hollow—that is if they are allowed to hold it. But we have to get your application from a Chevrolet Automobile dealership. Would you like to ride to Russellville to get one? I thought if you would; we'd make a day of it. I have some business with the *Courier Democrat* so my paper will pay for all of the expenses."

"Mr. Bell, I'll have to pay for the application."

"I don't think there is any charge for that. If there is, I'll front you the money, and you can pay me back. Anyway the rules say you can get sponsors to help you pay for the costs of building the vehicle. And, if you win, you'll have something like Northern Arkansas *Meteor-Fever* painted on both sides. Several busloads of well wishers from both towns will be going up there with us to whoop and holler you to victory."

"Then you better start making plans."

On the day Jesse and Spence went to Russellville, they, found to their profound dismay, it was also the day Rex and his father had decided to get their application.

Two shiny new cars stood on the showroom floor. Rex's father was holding an open door of one and Rex was inside gripping the steering wheel. A salesman walked to Rex's father and said, "Boy, she's a real honey. She has an automatic transmission, so there is no shifting gears, and a rear-view mirror on the door added to the one in the interior. There are lots more safety items, but the big selling feature of this baby is all the horses under the hood."

"I'm not looking to buy. We just came to get an application for next year's Soap Box Derby."

"You buy those at the gate."

"No. We don't want stadium tickets to see the race, my boy wants to race in it."

"I see. I'm not sure we have any applications. The closest race is Kansas City."

"There's going to be a local race in Skunk Hollow."

"You sure about that?"

"Reasonably. Derby officials have been there for several weeks during the building of the track."

"Well, hold tight. Let me see if I can help these other customers and then I'll check with my boss."

The salesman walked to the second of his display cars.

Jesse said, "How long have you had models for sale?"

"We got our first last year. Before that we were making vehicles for the war."

Jesse looked inside the second model then ran his hand down along the rear fender. "She sure is good-looking, but what the boy wants is an application for the Soap Box Derby."

Looking at Spencer, the salesman said, "You going to be racing in Skunk Hollow too."

"Yes, sir."

Jesse and Spencer turned their heads to see if Rex and his father had been listening. They were.

"I'll be right back. Why don't you look at these brochures, open the door, and sit behind the steering wheel—get a feel for it."

Rex and his father had walked away from their display model and were huddled in an animated conversation. In a moment, the father came over and introduced himself and Rex.

Jesse said, "I'm Jesse Bell, and this is Spencer from Dancing Deer. We came for the Grand Opening of your racetrack. It is quite impressive. And *The Wind* is impressive in its own right. Spencer here is looking forward to competing against it next summer."

Andy Muldoon looked at Spencer, "Have you ever built a racer?"

"No. But it shouldn't be too difficult."

Mr. Muldoon and his son turned toward each other. There was a silent moment then both exploded in laughter. They were still laughing when the salesman came back with two applications.

"Something funny?"

"Oh, no." Rex's father turned toward Jesse and Spencer. "Sorry, Spencer. We didn't mean to be rude. But for anyone to believe they can build a racer good enough to put up a fight against *The Wind*, is appraising the situation through rose-tinted glasses. Good luck." With that, he took one of the applications and walked out while Rex was wiping his eyes with a shirt sleeve.

Jesse put his hand on Spencer's shoulder as both watched Rex and Mr. Muldoon saunter out with their application. "I don't think those two know who they're up against."

CHAPTER 23 – SPENCER BEGINS ANEW
November, 1946

Spencer stared through the window as he rode in the cab of Gus' truck. He'd decided to take his racer to Edwin's garage where there were proper tools he could use in his makeover. There was no way his car, in its present state, would be competitive with that blue streak. It was a pivotal moment. In fact, there were several pivotal moments. The first was when they pulled off the covering revealing *The Wind*. What a magnificent car. It was more than a racing car—it was art. It was even more than that. It was a work of art engineered to fly. Seeing it fly was his second pivotal moment. Spencer wondered what it would be like to sit behind the steering wheel while *The Wind* grabbed hold of gravity and shot down the track.

"Son, what changes do you plan on making?"

"I haven't decided. Determination and stubbornness are my two greatest assets, but are they enough to overcome the monumental problem I've encountered? I'm not sure any car built by anybody can beat *The Wind*."

"You have to give it your best shot, Spence. Winning against *The Wind* might not be your ultimate achievement. Impressing someone who could help you become the engineer you hope to be might happen, or teaching yourself new skills you'll use later for a more important achievement, or, still yet, just learning more about what gives you that sense of determination and stubbornness might be in the cards."

"We'll see. I'm not giving up just because the bar has been placed so high."

"That's what I like to hear. And you know that you have a whole lot of people at your back. Edwin has been a good friend for a long time and, even though he can't help you build your racer, he'll be able to show you how to use his tools. And he may have some ideas of his own you could add to yours."

Gus pulled his truck into Edwin's drive and circled around the house to the garage. Edwin was sitting under a shade tree in a wheelchair drinking lemonade with his caretaker and adopted daughter.

"I see you didn't try to hide your racer from other possible competitors."

"Why would I want to do that?"

Laurie spoke, "That was my idea. I told Edwin that you didn't want anyone to see your racer because if they copied your original model and made one slight improvement you would be at a disadvantage."

"Yeah. That might have been accurate in the distant past but now the car to beat is not mine but the one down the road."

Gus lowered the tailgate and started untying the straps keeping Spencer's racer from sliding around the cargo bed. Spencer put a pair of two-by-sixes on the edge of the tailgate down to the ground. Edwin and the two girls watched as Gus and Spencer rolled the racer down the improvised ramps.

Laurie raised the garage door with Spencer pushing his car into the middle of its new construction site. The five attendees sat in a semi-circle of lawn-chairs and one wheelchair facing the object of their concern.

Laurie spoke first. "Spencer, what can we do to help?"

"I could use your advice. But I have to do the work myself."

"What kind of advice? We were all there when your main competition showed us what you're up against. So where are you in the development of something that can outpace *The Wind*?"

"I think I can use the existing platform and the steering and linkage assembly. But I have to have a more aerodynamic design."

Edwin asked, "What are the constraints?"

"Wind and friction."

"Okay. Let's make a wind-tunnel for determining air-flow. We can then reshape anything that restricts that flow. For the friction, I suppose that would be the wheel bearings, where the tire meets the road, and . . . and what else?"

"Not much. I have to use the wheels, axles, and bearings that came from Ohio in my package. They also sent me the steering mechanism. So every boy building a racer is on the same page."

Gus said, "Did the bearings come packed with grease?"

"Yeah, but they are made to be easily re-packed. I have to remember to check them before any race."

Laurie refilled Spencer's glass. She said, "When will you be starting?"

Spencer walked to the peg-board on the garage wall and took off a small crowbar. He then stood in front of the racer and said, "Right now."

For the rest of the afternoon, Spencer dismantled his racer while his four best fans watched in silence. Occasionally a comment was made but Spencer was focused and either did not feel the need to respond or did not the hear the comment in the first place. About four-thirty Gus said, "Boy, you need to start putting up Edwin's tools. It'll be dark soon, and we have chores to do before supper."

Spencer looked through a window and realized just how early the sun set in late November. He finished removing the steering wheel before gathering several tools to replace on the pegboard. Laurie stood at his side holding the few tools that remained.

Spencer took them from her and started replacing each one in its proper place on the wall. "Thank you, Laurie."

"Think nothing of it. I want you to win this race and feel bad I can't do more to help."

"At this point a little support goes a long way."

The next morning a work truck with "The Calhoun Construction Company" painted on its side arrived at Edwin's house with a load of lumber and a large floor-standing fan.

Laurie directed the two workers to unload the material and place it in a corner of the garage. When the two workers had left Laurie walked to the shade tree where Issie sat beside Edwin. "I suppose with the fan we're going to build Spencer a wind tunnel."

"We ought to help the boy any way we can, as long as we stay within the rules."

The next week was Thanksgiving and Spencer had already mentioned that he would not be able to work on the racer until the week after. So Laurie and Edwin felt they had a week to build the wind-tunnel before turning over their tools to Spencer.

Laurie drew the diagram on paper according to Edwin's instructions. From measuring the racer, they added a few inches for safety. It was a committee project with each arguing for their own infusion of ideas.

Issie said, "I think it ought to have wheels so we could push it around on the floor."

Laurie said, "If we used the one-by lumber instead of the two-by lumber it would be light enough Spencer and Gus could easily pick it up and place it wherever they wanted."

"I think we ought to have leather straps screwed into the four corners then we could slide in two poles through the straps and carry it around with the poles on our shoulders."

How are we going to determine how the wind flows. You can't see the wind?" said Issie. "And we can't use ashes, dye, or anything that might damage the racer's finish."

"How about smoke?" said Laurie. "And we need to have a white background so we can see that smoke."

"My goodness, you girls are making this so hard." said Edwin.

CHAPTER 24 – THE GANG

January, 1947

"Man, Rex your tree house is great. How 'bout letting me move in? I'd take care of it for you."

"You got to be kidding. I ain't got no bathroom, no electricity, no running water."

"Yeah, but look at what you do have. Your dad changed out the glass in the windows for sheets of clear plastic, you got a tent heater with plenty of kerosene, and your ladder slides up so no one can bother you if you want privacy. I ain't got nowhere I can go for privacy."

"Alvin, you got too many sisters in your family for privacy. Not only do your sisters know everything you do, but they talk about it at school. Nothing about you is private. I'm thinking seriously about asking you to leave while the rest of us plan our strategy."

"Please don't do that. If I don't say nothing, no one will know."

"Then how come your sisters know so much about you?"

"Cause they're snoopy, and I used to keep a diary."

"I thought only girls kept diaries."

"Yeah, last year one of them gave me a diary for Christmas and talked about how much fun it was to write down everything she did in hers that I tried it out. I enjoyed it too until I read in one of theirs how they were keeping up with my activities by sneaking peeks at mine."

"Okay, Alvin you can stay as long as you don't talk about what we're doing or write about it in your diary."

"Thanks. Will you pass me a cookie?"

"Has anyone found out about any other good racers being built?"

"Yeah, several boys in Skunk Hollow but none in the same category as *The Wind*. There are a few in Russellville, two in Clarksville, and some more in Dancing Deer. One in Russellville and another in Dancing Deer might give you trouble. The others are constructed poorly."

"The one in Dancing Deer made by someone named Spencer?"

"Yeah. How'd you know?"

"I've met him. He told me he was looking forward to racing *The Wind.*"

"He's building the *Orphan Express*. But we can't find it. I've located his house and looked through every inch of the barn. But, so far, we've only got rumors."

"Why'd he name it the *Orphan Express*?" said Rex.

"Not sure. That's not what he calls it. It's what everyone else calls it. They talk about it like he's finished and will use it to win easily against *The Wind*. It's supposed to have three speeds with the fastest of the three too scary for this Spencer kid to take a chance on. Some say the boy's a genius builder but no one has seen his car. It's all hush hush."

"Well, we better do something. I'll not be able to go to Akron if I can't win the local race here. What about the racer in Russellville?"

"Now that one I've seen. It looks like a giant cigar. The driver rides in it laying down and keeps up with his lane markers and the other cars by an elaborate arrangement of mirrors."

"How fast is it?"

"Pretty fast. It has limited wind resistance—no angles."

"What can we do?"

"Me and the boys have been thinking about that and have come up with a neat solution. The car is heavy, and the boy is pretty big himself. We thought about giving him all our extra Halloween candy. With a known sweet tooth, he probably won't make weight when time for the race rolls around."

"Okay, next time we meet, I want more information about the *Orphan Express* and an update on the Halloween candy ploy."

"You got it, boss."

Chapter 25 – THE GIRLS

January, 1947

"How many will there be in your party?"

"Three."

"Please, have a seat. I should have a table for you in a few minutes."

Sydney Rene looked at the two women standing to her right. "I knew it. We should have made reservations."

"Ma'am, we don't take reservations for lunch, only for the evening meal."

In a milder tone Trish whispered, "Sidney, he said it would only be a few minutes. We are not so important that he should give us preferential treatment. After all, I've had to wait for a table at Sacre Bleu—and that's my restaurant."

Beatrice said, "Your restaurant?"

"I feel like its mine. But then, I did talk you into opening it in the first place."

"Yes, you did. And I'll forever be grateful to you for making the suggestion."

The three women found comfortable seating and gawked at the nicely dressed men in attendance. One of the women was a tall woman wearing a blue beret. She said, "Have you noticed how many men are wearing coats and ties? Most of the men coming into my restaurant for lunch are wearing overalls and straw hats."

"There are other differences. At your restaurant, there are more women than men and here it's the other way around. I'll bet it's the decor. A man had to be in charge of decorating this place, and he made it friendly and comfortable in a manly sort of way. The Sacre Bleu is preferable to my tastes. It's more feminine and cozy. In the Sacre Bleu you have a man and a woman walking through singing love songs to each other—sometimes together, sometimes looking for each other, or sometimes trying to avoid one another. Some walls have nooks containing potted plants or sculptures; other walls are plastered with art. Love is in the air at Sacre Bleu; this place is all about business."

"Maybe so, but the food is supposed to be as good, or better than, mine."

"That's what we're here to find out. And three attractive, single ladies should not have to wait until some man wants to take a moment of his time to find us a place to sit."

"Calm down, Sydney. This just gives us an opportunity to appraise the situation. Besides, someone may want us to join him. In fact, I see someone heading our way right now."

Jesse Bell walked up and held out his hand to Patricia Kilburn. "Miss Kilburn, would you and your two friends care to join me. I have a table all to myself."

"Thank you, Mr. Bell. Let me introduce you to Sydney Rene Thompkins and Beatrice Baxter."

"Ladies, I personally want to welcome you to Dancing Deer. Is there any special occasion, I'm not aware of, happening today? I mean something must be going on for the three most beautiful women in Skunk Hollow to grace us with their presence."

"No. We're just out shopping and wanted to get out of the hustle and bustle of life in the big city."

"Do you think that census was taken accurately. I mean Dancing Deer has always been the bigger of the . . ."

"Hello, Jesse. You must introduce me."

"Bill, I've invited these lovely ladies to have their lunch with me. It seems all of the tables are full."

"Nonsense. My personal table will seat six and besides it's next to a window overlooking Main Street. I'll tell the maître de to prepare it for us. Ladies, my name is Bill Potter—I own the Ritz Grand Hotel and Ballroom and this little restaurant."

After a little mumbling, Jesse did get the introductions made. The maître de had two waiters arrange the chairs at Bill's table with another waiter bringing a beverage and salad already delivered to Jesse's table.

Trish Kilburn said, "And you own the bank in town."

"Quite right."

"So, you are the detestable, Bill Potter?"

"I've been called worse."

"Andre, you'll never guess who's here."

"Who's here, Gerald?"

"That tall woman with the flashing eyes who's got your life going topsy-turvy."

"She's here?"

"Yep. Waiting for a table."

Andre ran to the mirror on the wall he had placed there for his female employees. He removed his chef's hat, ran his fingers through his hair, and twirled his mustache. "Gerald finish this chocolate dessert, will you; I'm going to help her find a table and may have my meal on the floor."

"Sure, boss."

Andre walked through two swinging doors, recognized a volatile situation happening at the owner's table, and grabbed the menus from under the arm of a hesitating waiter. "I'll take care of this for you."

At Bill's table, a woman stood holding a butter knife in a threatening manner. "Please, Mademoiselle. Let me prepare something special for you. Mr. Potter has already eaten and can't stay."

"You are so right, Andre." Bill stood at his chair, "Ladies, enjoy your meal. I have to be going." Bill did not turn to walk away but backed up six feet before making his escape.

Sydney sat down, took a drink of water, then said, "Potter almost put our bank out of business. My family thinks he is related to the devil somehow."

"What did he do? It must have happened after I had to give all of my bank shares back to your dad."

Trish said, "Why'd you have to do that, Beatrice?"

"It's a sad story. I came back to marry Asa and then my father came into my room and said the marriage was off. Under no circumstances would he allow me to marry into that despicable family. I cried for two weeks. But what I want to know is what did Mr. Potter do?"

"I'm not sure I know everything, but I . . . Mr. Bell, isn't there some other place you'd rather be?"

"Not really. However, I will go back to my table if you'll give me an exclusive interview if you shoot someone today."

"Jesse, I've already got dibs on that."

"I guess I'll have to read about it your *Skunk Hollow Fever* then."

"And as for you, Monsieur," Beatrice smiled at Andre, "Please prepare three plates of whatever you're most famous for."

"It will be my pleasure. And it is so nice to see you again, Mademoiselle." Andre bowed in Beatrice's direction before leaving.

The three women leaned forward with their heads close to the center of the table. Sydney continued with, "In '31, we had a run on the bank; scared people lined up at our bank's doors—and Potter's as well—wanting their money. At the head of the line in front of our bank was Bill Potter wanting his money. When we gave it to him, there wasn't enough left to pay the good people in Skunk Hollow. The scoundrel took our money and paid off the people in line at his bank.

"Then Bill Potter was tried for killing a prostitute and a traveling man passing through his town. Asa thought it was a good time to open a branch of our bank in Dancing Deer. But Potter demanded our bank give him back money he had deposited. It seems he had more money deposited with us—this time he had opened an account using his middle name. And when it took us a couple of days to get it together he used that as proof we couldn't be trusted with anybody's money. Then he bought the building we were renting and evicted us. When word got out, no one had enough nerve to rent to us, so we had to pack up and go home."

"How did you get through? asked Trish.

"For the run on the bank Dad borrowed money from Beatrice's father by putting our house and land up as collateral. And, when we couldn't pay Dane Baxter back, he foreclosed giving Beatrice our home to appease her for not letting her marriage to Asa take place. For the fiasco of our branch bank in Dancing Deer, Asa got sacked. Dad then asked Howdy to take over."

Trish said, "I can understand bringing in Howdy, but, for the earlier problem, why didn't your dad take the deed to his house and land to some other bank to get the money to pay off Beatrice's father?"

"I don't know."

"I do."

Trish Kilburn and Sidney Thompkins turned to look at Beatrice. Sidney said, "Well, I would like to know, but first, I think you ought to be told that Asa really does love you. He doesn't date anyone or have much interest in anything. Actually, the man lives in a small apartment in downtown Skunk Hollow. He ran for mayor because Howdy told him to, or he'd not come manage our bank. But, other than the few activities he does for the town as the mayor, he sits by himself in a dark apartment wondering how he ever let his only love get away."

Trish said, "That is so sad."

Both girls looked at Beatrice for any pieces of the puzzle not yet known.

Beatrice cleared her throat, "When my grandfather Woodrow settled here with half of the money from one of the two saddlebags, he tried to buy the bank. He had already bought the land and had put money back for the building of our house and damming up a stream for the Lake of the Beatrice. With the amount of money he had left there wasn't enough to buy the bank. And the Butler's weren't willing to finance any part of the purchase price.

"Then he got the letter from Albert saying he'd had his money stolen. My grandfather went to help Albert and ended up getting back most of what had been stolen. When they arrived in Skunk Hollow, Albert lived at our house for a while. In fact, he liked our house so much that he asked my grandfather to sell him all of our land across the lake.

"My grandfather knew how much money Albert had so when Albert bought the bank my grandfather got a pencil and figured how much Albert had remaining after purchasing the three hundred acres and setting aside a whopping large amount to build the house.

Now Albert bought sixty percent with my grandfather buying fifteen percent and the remaining twenty-five percent was divided by three other people. Grandfather determined that Albert should have been short by two hundred thousand dollars. As part of the agreement by which my father bailed out the bank, your father had to tell mine where Albert got the additional funds."

"And?"

"It seems that when they divvied up the cash in the first saddlebag there was gold hidden in the second. Half of that should have been given to my grandfather as well. Sydney, your father agreed. So when your dad couldn't pay he signed over the deed to your house and land and my father countered by handing over his fifteen percent of the bank."

Nothing was said for several minutes then Andre arrived with a rolling cart saying he was planning on preparing the meal at their table.

CHAPTER 26 – THE WHEEL

February, 1947

Spencer arrived at Edwin's house around 8:00 a.m. Snow had fallen during the night so Gus's livestock would be spending the day inside the barn and small paddock. When this happens, Spencer gets his chores accomplished in a shorter time span. But, he used the extra minutes walking into town instead of riding his bicycle. May made him wear extra clothing. There was no way he could ride the bike with all the layers of clothing he now wore.

Edwin had given Spencer a key after Laurie spotted foreign footprints after a rain. Nothing was missing, but Edwin started locking his workshop at night. He and Spencer were the only ones with keys.

After opening the door, Spencer went straight to the fire. Soon the shop would be warm enough he could remove the extra layers of clothing. After starting the fire, Spencer walked to his racer and noticed one flap had been raised like someone was curious to know what lay hidden but failed to make the flap fall to the floor after inspecting. Spencer thought he must not have positioned it properly himself and proceeded to remove and fold the entire covering.

Laurie came inside the workshop with two cups of hot chocolate. She gave one to Spencer and then pulled up a comfortable chair close to the fire. "I told Gladys to bring my breakfast out here. She fixes pancakes on Saturdays. Would you like some?

"I'll tell her you do, because, when you smell mine, with sweet maple syrup, there is no way you can continue to hold out. And, if you don't eat them, someone else will."

"Laurie, are you happy here?"

"Now, what kind of silly question is that? Of course, I'm happy here. They don't treat me like a child but as an adult who needs a lot of explaining. And I earn my keep by entertaining Edwin. Quite an easy assignment. You might say I stepped into a honey bucket."

"I'm glad. Actually, I haven't heard anyone complain about the family adopting them. Gus and May always wanted children but didn't think they could afford the expense. Millie and I have tried to make their lives easier. Millie starts doing housework the moment she arrives home from school, then she helps May cook supper and washes the dishes before starting her homework, and I do everything outside. There's no complaining, no wondering what could have been had we been adopted by wealthier parents. No, we're as happy as pigs in new mud.

So, your dream of being an engineer is in jeopardy because the cost of your schooling is out of Gus and May's budget and it wouldn't if they were wealthier? And you're not upset about that?"

"Not in the least. If I don't win the Soap Box Derby, I'll try something else, and look at everything I've learned and the friends I've made."

"That's true." Laurie got up from her chair and went to the back of Spencer's car. "Spence, look at this back tire. It's crooked."

"Let me see that. Oh, no. It's warped. Now how could that have happened? I imagine a sudden change in temperature might have done it." Spencer removed the wheel and held it under a light. "Here, Laurie, look at this. It has parallel marks on both sides like it was squeezed tight in a vise. I didn't notice that when I first installed it. I'll have to buy a new one."

"How much will a new wheel cost you?"

"More than I have. And there are no jobs in the winter. I'll have to think of something."

Spencer sat in a chair looking into space. In a moment he said, "Do you know what happens when someone sponsors a racer?"

"No. Where'd you hear that?"

"Mr. Bell, at the *Meteor*. He said I could get sponsors to help with the cost of building the car, but I have to do all the labor myself."

"Spencer, you build the car and I'll get you those sponsors."

CHAPTER 27 – THE SPONSORS
March, 1947

"Good morning, Mr., Creighton. I have the drawings I've made for your jewelry store. All you have to do is pick out the one you want. And the next time you see Spencer parading around town with the *Orphan Express*, posing to have his picture taken for the *Marsden County Meteor*, or just making a public appearance you'll see him sporting your patch. Also, the *Orphan Express* will be displaying your name for all to know that Creighton Jewelry is helping Spencer and his racer win the derby at Skunk Hollow."

"How many sponsors have you got, Laurie?"

"Five. You will make number six—the final one. Mr. Creighton, for a measly fifty dollars you will get to have your picture taken standing beside Spencer when the officials in Skunk Hollow present him with the trophy. You will be able to sit at the winner's table at the new bewitching French cafe, Sacre Bleu, in Skunk Hollow after the presentation. And you and your wife will get to ride on the sponsor's float right behind Spencer and the *Orphan Express* in the Dancing Deer Victory Parade. That will be the day after the final race. Additionally, for another twenty dollars per appearance Spencer will bring the *Orphan Express* into your store to give autographs and make a speech to your customers."

"What if he doesn't win?"

"In that unlikely scenario, Spencer will have done his best; you and five friends will have had a say, but some other worthy opponent will represent northern Arkansas in Akron, Ohio. Mr. Creighton, a best effort is all that anyone can expect. Of course, Spencer will be crestfallen and Dancing Deer will go through a period of mourning, but if Spencer loses, he will be the first to congratulate the champion—and I think you'll want to be a part of that."

"Young lady; indeed I do. And if you ever need a job in sales I hope you'll see me about a job."

"Mr. Creighton, do you see a drawing you like. Originally his racer was going to be British racing green but to show off the sponsors' insignias with a burst of color I've been able to get him to change to pearlescent white. I think a good color for you would be bright orange. And I could make the rays going out from the diamond to be yellow—like the sun."

"I like it. I like it. And I want to pay for two appearances at my store. Is there any way I could pay extra and get preferential treatment when you choose the placement of the insignia?"

"As long as its the same size as the other sponsors' logos."

"I can agree with that. Let me get my checkbook."

CHAPTER 28 – LYDIA
March, 1947

Lydia stood in line at the cafeteria beside her best friend, Sally Benton. "Sally, you need to eat more vegetables."

"Nonsense. I like sweets."

"Horsefeathers."

"Hey, Lydia. Have you heard what the boys will be doing this weekend?"

"No. Is it anything out of the ordinary?"

"Not for them. There are two racers they think will be good enough to give *The Wind* a run for its money so they're making a trip tonight to Russellville and tomorrow night to Dancing Deer to do something to sabotage those possibilities."

"Does Rex know?"

"Yeah. He's the one who's asked the boys to take care of the competition."

"And the boys are?"

"They are my brother, Alvin, and his two best friends, Don and Proctor. Proctor is going to steal his father's car. They're supposed to pick up Alvin at midnight so they can do their dirty work while everyone is asleep."

"How do you know this Sally? Did Alvin brag about it?"

"I have my ways. Alvin has never been able to keep anything from me. I know everything there is to know about that boy."

That evening Lydia helped her mother set the table for supper. "Mom, if you know somebody is doing wrong to someone else would you intervene in some way?"

"Probably not. When I was your age, it was usually me doing the something wrong. And if someone told on me then that person was my enemy and I wouldn't have anything to do with her."

"But what if you liked the person doing the wrong? Isn't there something I can do to make him not do the wrong?"

"A boy? Who are you talking about, Lydia?"

"It's no one. I was just wondering how I can determine what is the right decision to make. Yesterday I saw a girl cheat on a spelling test. And I couldn't decide whether to tell the teacher or not. How does a person decide questions like that?"

"Honey, I think you'd have to decide based on the outcome of telling versus not telling. I mean, would you be harmed in any way if you let the girl get away with cheating. If you did tell someone would there be repercussions against you by the girl, her big, mean brother, or her family? And you have to consider the seriousness of the offence. Cheating on a spelling test is not near as serious as lying to a police officer or stealing."

"So, Mom, you're saying if I am not wronged and the severity of the crime is minor, I should just mind my own business. Or, if I would suffer from the wrong and would not be hurt from informing an authority then I should present my evidence. Or, if I could be injured by retaliation from my telling, but it was also me who had to suffer the wrong then it would depend on the severity."

"Lydia, my dear, you are analyzing this too much. Those thoughts will go through your mind in a split second. And I trust you to make the right decision.

"Now, go call your brother for supper."

After washing the dishes while her brother dried and replaced them in the cabinet, Lydia went into the hallway and called Rex. "Rex, I heard today that someone was going to damage two racers they thought might be stiff competition for *The Wind*. That wasn't your idea was it?"

"Certainly not. Who told you?"

"I can't say. But I told them you had nothing to do with it. You are too good a person to act in such a childish manner."

"You got that right. But if you would tell me who is saying those dreadful things about me I could take care of it myself."

"Rex, no one said you were involved. Just that three boys would be doing their part to help a Skunk Hollow racer win against a car from Russellville and another from Dancing Deer."

"Did this person say who the three boys were?"

"Yeah, they've been bragging about it to their friends and someone overheard. I hope you're smart enough not to associate with boys like them."

"Lydia, thanks for the heads up. I don't know who the three boys could be, but I'll keep my ears open. I'm sure glad I'm not implicated in any way. You're sure I'm not, right?"

"I think so. But you know how rumors go. Someone hears a rumor and wonders who would benefit then wonders if the person benefitted is involved. The next person hearing the rumor finds out the benefiting person is probably the instigator. And as the rumor goes around it becomes magnified and the crime, and the conspiracy to commit the crime, gets more embellished. And the next thing you know the police come to your doorstep in the middle of the night flashing their badges and holding a warrant for your arrest."

"Holy cow. I am so frosted."

CHAPTER 29 – THE CITY COUNCIL
March, 1947

Mayor Bob folded his paper. "George, the citizens of Dancing Deer are upset. Skunk Hollow is hulking in the shadows waiting for their chance while we idle away our time with tiresome chit-chat. What we need is to wake up and get back in the forefront of things."

"Mayor Bob, I for one, need some good press for a change."

"Well, you ain't getting any. Skunk Hollow is getting all the good press. They've garnered this Soap Box Derby racing thing bringing in a thousand or more people to spend money. They got new shops on every corner. They got a new restaurant my wife has been begging me to take her to. And they now have a newspaper to tell everybody how wonderful life is in the pleasant little community of Skunk Hollow."

George Satterfield raised his hand. In a matter of seconds, a waitress appeared with a pot of coffee. After she left, George said, "I wasn't going to run for another term, but when Summer turned in her application, people started asking if I was afraid of being trounced by my wife in the next election."

"Yeah, me too," said Faisal Obadiah.

"So, what are we going to do? Election is in November and we can't get our names in the paper for any commendable activity. And, not only that, but the women have been boning up on all things political."

"That is so weird," said Mayor Bob.

"What's weird?"

"Listening to Clarice talk about the tax base, funding new projects, salary levels in the police department, instituting a new hotel tax, and parking meters. I want my wife back not this politically savvy mayoral candidate getting ready to . . . to . . ."

"Go ahead say it. We're all in the same boat."

"Oh man, I don't want to lose my job as mayor to my wife. That would be more than humiliating."

Faisal said, "Okay, let's do something for the town that'll get the voters thinking we're doing a grand job. Anyone got any ideas?"

"Let's give them a party."

"Yeah, and while we're at it, let's convince Bill that it was his idea and that he needs to supply the place and all the food."

"What kind of party?"

"That race is coming up. How many boys in Dancing Deer are building a racer?"

"I've heard five applications have been submitted, but only three boys have been mentioned around town. There's Big John Lynch's grandson, Toby, and that kid who rode his horse down the sidewalk. And one of the orphans, Spencer, I think."

"Okay, here's what we do. We rope off one of the streets and let our boys display their new racers. Even let them ride a piece. We'll have a country hoedown in town to celebrate their efforts—carry them around on our shoulders like they're heroes or something."

George said, "Those racers don't have motors. They operate on gravity. To run they have to be going downhill."

"George, we don't have any hills in town. The only slope we got is highway 27 leaving town."

Mayor Bob continued with, "That's still good. Let's run the race from out on Highway 27 into town. Then when they get off we'll feed them homemade ice cream."

"Sounds like a party to me. It's got a car race, town celebrities, ice cream, hay ride, and a country hoedown."

"Where'd the hayride come from?"

"I just threw that in in case some of the town folk need a lift out to the start of the race."

"Hey, have either of you responded to that reporter from Skunk Hollow?"

"What reporter?"

"The one that wanted to interview the three members of the city council having to run against their wives if they want to stay in office. He thinks we should have a debate."

"Okay. Let's use city funds to pay for the party and do it up right. You know balloons, flyers, and plenty of food."

CHAPTER 30 – THE ORPHAN EXPRESS
March, 1947

Spencer stepped back for a better look. His first car was boxy compared to the one now standing on his work table. It had been an arduous process. First the wind tunnel built by Edwin and the girls didn't work. Their intention was good, but what they ended up with was a monstrosity that didn't work. It was too big, too heavy, and too difficult to color the wind so he could see how it flowed around the car.

Spencer did not want to make anybody mad so he tinkered with the apparatus, Edwin expressed his ideas, and the girls got their hammers, screwdrivers, and chisels flying. Before long the entire mess occupied a pile in the corner of the shop with each participant expressing sorrow the contraption didn't work.

Then Laurie had a brilliant idea. They'd make a smaller version—this time in a large shoebox. For the racer, Spencer could mold it out of clay. Then he could place it in a shoebox and blow the water vapor from a block of dry ice at it.

Further adjustments had to be made. First the fan had to be small. It needed to be the same diameter as his model. Then the wall of the box behind the racer had to be covered with an absorbent sheet of paper. The better the racer's design, the smaller the affected area on the paper. Pretty soon Spencer had made major modifications by using a scalpel to slice away unwanted parts of his clay car. When he was satisfied that the air was passing over his racer with the least amount of turbulence, he stood back and clicked his tongue against the roof of his mouth while holding his head sideways.

Laurie said, "Spence, are you seeing what I'm seeing?"

"Probably."

Edwin said, "I don't believe it."

Issie said, "I don't see anything out of the ordinary. What is it everyone is seeing?"

"Spencer's built a model that looks exactly like *The Wind*."

"So."

Edwin said, "It looks like someone designed *The Wind* using a wind tunnel just like you. That's probably why it's so fast."

"Okay, if this is the best design, we'll both use it."

For the next two weeks, Spencer designed a lightweight framework of slender pieces of wood. Then he started gluing on thin sheets of plywood that had been soaking in water and were semi-pliable for bending.

"Laurie, this would not have been possible had you not got the sponsors. There is no way I could have come up with the money necessary to buy the materials. Every time I turn around I need something else."

"It's been my pleasure. You've done a good job, Spence. As soon as you get the body finished and painted, I'll stencil on the Sponsor's names and logos and repaint over the stencils with bright colors. Adding advertising is not part of the building process is it?"

That Saturday night, just after midnight, a hand pried open a window with a slender young boy slipping through. In moments, a side door had been unlocked with two more boys joining the one who came through the window. With flashlights, they pulled back a canvas cover to discover the *Orphan Express*.

"What do you think we ought to do? It needs to be something not readily apparent. Something that will slow it down just a bit. Or something he can't easily fix."

"Or we could do something that if he does win he'd get disqualified for."

"We've already talked about that and so far no one has come up with an idea that works. I think we need to do something to the racer that costs him more to fix than he has money to cover."

"I've got it. Let's remove the screw holding on the steering wheel. And use a hacksaw to cut it leaving one thread, then replace the nut. We could then take the cut part of the screw to back into the nut from the outside. He wouldn't think to take it back apart and when he drives in his first race the steering wheel will come off in his hand and the car will crash or veer into his competitor's lane. If he doesn't crash, he'll be disqualified."

"That's brilliant."

CHAPTER 31 – SHOWING OFF

April, 1947

With six weeks before the local race in Skunk Hollow, the citizens of Dancing Deer wanted to celebrate the arrival of Spring by showcasing their entries into the upcoming derby. The only hill of any note was on Highway 27 leaving town toward Cakebread. Or, as someone noted, arriving into town from Cakebread. So the county sheriff planned to block off the portion outside the city limits and the local constabulary had made arrangements to block off the finish within the city proper. It was not a long distance, but it did cover the entire down-hill spiral.

Laurie put on the last of the six logos with the one for Creighton Jewelry in a prominent position just below Spencer's name. She had asked the authorities in Skunk Hollow if adding the logos could be done by someone other than the boy building the racer and had received a positive reply.

Laurie said, "Spencer, do you think the two curves will make the racers keep their speed down?"

"Naw, besides we're not racing, just showing off our workmanship."

"Mr. Creighton asked if you could display the *Orphan Express* in his showroom for three days prior to the celebration. He's got a big sale planned."

"It's ready. I've done everything I could. And, I have to admit, the pearlescent white paint looks pretty classy with those fancy advertisements. No one's going to get into the car are they?"

"We'll tell Mr. Creighton to rope it off. The car is on display and no one should be touching it."

On Wednesday afternoon, Gus and Spencer pushed the *Orphan Express* out of Edwin's workshop and onto the bed of Gus's old truck."

"I feel bad about delivering the racer in my truck. This is the first time anyone has seen it, except for Jesse and that girl he had tagging along writing down everything you said. I understand there is a mob of people outside Mr. Creighton's store waiting on us. And here we are bringing the pride of the entire town in a beat-up old pickup."

"Gus, did you wash it?"

"Yep. And cleaned out the interior and swept the bed."

"You know, someone will probably make you an offer to buy. Farmers everywhere are looking for decent work trucks."

"You think."

Spencer swelled with pride as they coasted down main street. People on the sidewalk stopped to see the racer everyone was talking about. There were three racers built in Dancing Deer but the other two paled in comparison to the one built by an aspiring engineer, the boy who walked into town bringing back the town's money two year's prior, and the same boy who carried his little sister into St. Bartholomew's Catholic Orphanage three years prior to that.

"Spencer, would you like to see the other two racers? They put one on display at the livery Feed and Seed and the second is in the lobby of the bank."

"Maybe later."

Gus parked directly in front of Creighton's Jewelry. He and Spencer unloaded the *Orphan Express* with several people wanting an up-close look. Mr. Creighton stood in front of two opened front doors. A photographer from the *Meteor* took pictures and a reporter followed Spencer and the racer asking questions as he walked.

"How long did you work on the *Orphan Express*?"

"Almost a year."

"And this is your first Soap Box Derby racer?"

"Yes, sir."

"Is it as fast as *The Wind*?"

"That will be determined in June in Skunk Hollow. But there are other racers that stand a good chance. However, everyone thinks the one to beat is *The Wind*."

"How long will your racer be on display?"

"Until the morning of our town celebration on Saturday."

Mr. Creighton turned to the crowd gathering around Spencer and the car. He opened his arms and welcomed everyone into his store. "The *Orphan Express* will be on display for three days and my store is having its biggest sale of the year. For those of you who want your picture taken standing beside our star attraction please get in line. You might have to wait a short while, the paper wants its shots first."

Mr. Creighton turned to the photographer. "Please make sure my logo is in focus."

"Yes, sir."

After having his picture taken a dozen or more times and answering a thousand questions and receiving a promise not to let anyone sit in his car Spencer left with Gus. Spencer wanted to check out the hill where he would first test his car. All of the derby races were on straightaways, but this stretch of highway included two curves.

It was not supposed to be a race—more like a parade, but Spencer planned on winning just the same. And, in order to win, he thought he should travel the road looking for problem areas.

Gus drove slowly to allow Spencer a close inspection. Several times Spencer asked Gus to stop while he exited the truck for a look at a pothole or some other potential hazard. When Spencer was satisfied they went back to Edwin's workshop to make sure all the tools had been properly replaced, to load up any excess material used in the racer's construction, to accumulate the trash, and to sweep the floor.

While they were tidying up, Spencer sat down on a lawn chair. He put his head in his hands and said, "I bet no one thought about that."

"Thought about what?"

"Gus, did you notice how long the road was?"

"Yeah. Pert near a mile."

"The Derby Race Track in Akron, Ohio is eight hundred feet and the one in Skunk Hollow is a thousand feet but this one is five times the length of either of those."

"So, you'll have that much more of a leisurely drive."

"Gus, gravity builds on itself. At twenty feet, you're going faster than at ten feet and at forty feet you're going faster than you were at twenty and so on. At five thousand feet it could be dangerous."

"I don't think the city council would let the race happen if it were dangerous."

"You're probably right. There were stretches in the road where the gradient was almost nil. That should slow us down and I didn't see any part of the road with an excessive downhill slope. I guess it will be all right."

CHAPTER 32 – THE PRE-RACE PARADE

Late April, 1947

The Dancing Deer City Council chose the last Saturday in April to celebrate the coming of Spring and the entry of three Dancing Deer racers into the All American Soap Box Derby local race in Skunk Hollow.

Jesse Bell, the owner of the *Marsden County Meteor*, had been to a convention for small town newspaper editors in Baton Rouge, Louisiana and had only returned to Dancing Deer the morning of the race. Midge had prepared her boss a comfortable lawn chair halfway between the food tables and the finish line. When Jesse arrived, he had brought his mother and wife. Midge had to scramble for the extra seating, but, like most accomplished assistants, she was able to get the job done in an efficient time span.

Most of the town had gathered under shade trees and behind bales of hay. The hay was supposed to work as a barrier to keep the onlookers away from the action at the finish line and any out-of-control racers away from the spectators. Close to the finish line, and to the bales of hay, sat Edwin and Issie, his caretaker; Laurie, his adopted daughter; and Gladys, his wife. Next to Edwin, and his family, sat Gus and May Poindexter, the Dancing Deer family who adopted Millie and Spencer. Gus and Edwin were great friends as were May and Gladys. Millie and Laurie sat closer still to the bales of hay.

The two girls left to bring glasses of iced tea while Spencer shifted from one foot to another.

Gus said, "What's the matter Spence? You're acting like you've asked your dog to attack a cougar."

"I should have come out here last night and given the road a run. I have no idea if the wheels will stay on, if the steering wheel will turn the wheels, or if the brake will stop us after making it to the finish line."

"A lot of potential problems there. Are you thinking of backing out?"

"Certainly not. I'm just worried I might not have resolved all the problems."

"Spence, at some point you have to say you've done all you could. It's now time to see if it was enough."

"You're right. I'm headed to the top of the hill. Come on Gus, it's time."

Three thousand people gathered on the four corners of the intersection of Highway 27 going north to Cakebread and Main Street. Another three hundred people milled around the beginning of the race at the summit of a nice-sized hill just on the outskirts of town. Spencer and Gus jumped on a slow moving trailer already loaded with six passengers sitting on bales of hay. The trailer was pulled by a red International Harvester tractor to the starting point. No other vehicles were allowed on the highway.

To an elderly fellow passenger Spencer said, "This the last trip for spectators?"

"No. They got one more."

"Good. I didn't want to be late."

"One of those racers yours?"

"Yeah."

"You Wylie Santos, the kid who rode his horse on the sidewalk? I heard you had everyone running into the street."

Another rider said, "You must be new in town. This is Spencer. When that man shot Edwin and robbed Potter's bank, Spencer is the kid who brought the money back—a satchel full of money."

"The boxy looking thing, the one real skinny, or that snazzy white one everyone's been gawking at?"

Spencer said, "The white one. It's called the *Orphan Express*. I just hope it drives as good as it looks."

Like most town parties, everything needed was supplied in abundance. There was a good reason for the celebration, local heroes in attendance, tons of food, clear weather, and town politicians trying to put something in the plus column prior to running for re-election. Mayor Bob gave a speech. City Councilmen George Satterfield and Faisal Obadiah, over a loudspeaker, interviewed each of the racing drivers as they sat in their cars. And Makepeace Kilburn was there with his Leica camera to take photographs for the *Skunk Hollow Fever* newspaper. Jesse Bell for the *Marsden County Meteor*, had two photographers taking pictures, three reporters gathering interviews and public opinion, and had successfully evaded several women looking for press coverage to counter their husband's political coup.

"Spence, get in your car. I'll push you to the starting post. She sure is a beauty, but I don't think she's an orphan. The entire town is claiming her as theirs."

"I hope they'll still feel that way if I can't pull the upset."

"Spence, you just have to do your best."

"Ladies and gentlemen, in the first racer we have Toby Lynch in his *Screaming Eagle*. Toby, you understand this is not a race. When you're ready, take her for a pleasure stroll down the highway."

Toby raised his hand, and Big John Lynch gave his grandson's racer a gentle shove to get it going. There was ample applause from the three hundred or so gathered at the starting post.

Mayor Bob looked at racer number two, "Wylie, Wylie Santos, ladies and gentlemen. Give him a good old Dancing Deer thank you for all his hard work. Let's see, your racer is named *Hillbilly Hobo*. Take her to town, son and be safe."

"Ladies and gentlemen, our last racer is the *Orphan Express*. I'm sure everyone has read the articles in the paper about her construction and Jesse's interview with Spencer. When you're ready, Spencer raise your hand and Gus will shove you into the street."

Spencer's ears were still ringing with the town's pride expressed in loud clapping and a few whistles. Spencer wondered what their town mayor was using for brains. Surely he could figure out that the driver did not have control over how fast his car sailed down the track.

Spencer patted the *Orphan Express*, "Let's see what you got, girl."

Spencer's car rolled slowly the first twenty feet. Gradually its speed increased as it kept rolling down the gradient. At a hundred feet Spencer started to get sick to his stomach, he had realized there was no slowing down. At a hundred and fifty feet Spencer gauged his speed at twenty-five miles per hour. That was only ten miles per hour below the maximum victory speed limit posted for automobiles. He was wondering where were the level spots. At two hundred and fifty feet

Spencer was sure he had reached the maximum speed he could drive the *Orphan Express* and feel safe doing so. He still had five thousand feet to go and two curves. To slow things down, he began zigzagging the road. At a thousand feet, Spencer thought he had to be traveling sixty miles per hour. He started to look for a spot to bail.

At the finish line in town Genevieve asked, "Jesse, do you see the racers yet?"

"Not yet, honey. Let me get out the binoculars. It looks like Santos' *Hillbilly Hobo* has just passed Toby in his *Screaming Eagle*. Here comes the *Orphan Express*. It looks like Spencer is trying to keep from passing the other two by going back and forth on the road instead of driving in a straight line. Uh oh, the *Hillbilly Hobo* went into the ditch. I don't see him. He must've crashed."

Genevieve said, "Give me those binoculars." She snatched them away from Jesse, then said, "Jesse, I can't see a thing."

Jesse took the glasses back. He said, "The *Hillbilly Hobo* must've traveled in the ditch for a while because he's now back on the road. The *Orphan Express* has taken the lead. It looks like Toby has lowered his brake. It's slowed him down some. That must be dangerous traveling so fast with your foot pushing a padded stick against the pavement."

"Is the lead car the *Orphan Express*?"

"Yeah, but the *Hillbilly Hobo* is right on his tail. Uh oh, Wylie's back in the ditch. I guess he's using the grass and weeds to slow down. Wylie is a pretty smart boy."

Spencer was pinned against the seat. He didn't have to worry any longer if his car was fast. He now knew that achievement had been accomplished. Right now he was coming up on the first curve at an unbelievable speed with no brakes. This was not looking good. Then it happened. His steering wheel came off in his hand.

"The *Hillbilly Hobo* is back in the ditch. Oops, he got out just before running into a road sign. I don't see Toby's car. Spencer is standing up in the *Orphan Express*. He's got his steering wheel in his hand. Oh, no. There he goes. He couldn't make the curve."

"Here, take these. I've got to call an ambulance."

"Shouldn't there be one here already?" Genevieve was talking to an empty chair.

In two minutes, Wylie Santos in the *Hillbilly Hobo* came to the intersection where three thousand people had accumulated to slow down the runaway racers. Big Bear Radisson stopped Wylie by himself as the other spectators jumped out of the way after giving their desire to help a second thought.

Wylie sat in his car trying to collect his wits. Then Big Bear Radisson reached in and helped Wylie out. The boy had wobbly legs and looked spaced-out in a disoriented sort of way. He then fell to the pavement and kissed it.

Mayor Bob, the bull, ran up to Wylie. "Son, you okay?"

Wylie's mother was hugging her boy. She turned to the mayor. "Robert, this is all your fault. You did a poor job planning. The race was too long, the road too steep, and neither one of these boys had actually ridden their racers. You are an ignoramus. I'm voting for Clarice in the next election." She then started hitting Mayor Bob with her purse.

"Hilda, hit him one more time for me." The second woman turned to a man with a camera. "Did you get a picture of that? Who are you anyway?"

"Makepeace Kilburn from the *Skunk Hollow Fever*, ma'am." He looked up the road. "Where are the other two boys?"

The mayor looked down while shrugging his shoulders, "They crashed. The *Screaming Eagle* lost a wheel and the *Orphan Express* didn't make the curve. Spencer took it on a ride down the mountainside until he hit a tree. They're putting him in an ambulance right now."

When Big Bear Radisson heard that Spencer had wrecked, he jumped over the bales of hay and ran parallel to the road on the side of the mountain where he had last seen Spencer.

When he arrived at the crash site two medics had Spencer lying on the ground. After the medics checked to see if Spencer had any broken bones, they loaded him onto a stretcher and carried him up the mountainside to their waiting ambulance.

Big Bear was helpless. Spencer looked so pitiful Bear was heartbroken just looking at the proud young boy who had been brought to his knees by an ill-planned race.

Big Bear Radisson turned the broken racer right-side up, placed Spencer's helmet and goggles inside, then hefted the entire mess in his arms. It took him thirty minutes to carry the racer to the intersection.

CHAPTER 33 – LYDIA'S VISIT

Early May, 1947

Makepeace's article in the *Skunk Hollow Fever* included two pictures. The first was of the three boys standing beside their racers and the second of a boy being carried to an ambulance on a stretcher.

Lydia took the paper to the telephone and called Rex. "Have you seen the paper?"

"Yeah."

"Do you think you're gonna get away with it?"

"With what? I didn't do anything."

"Rex, I've heard three boys were instructed by you to sabotage two racers: one in Dancing Deer and the other in Russellville. All your boys did in Russellville was give up their Halloween candy. Now the racer with the driver can't make weight, but the boy in Dancing Deer got his car messed with. What did your guys do to Spencer's steering wheel?"

"Lydia, I don't know anything about that."

"You can't lie to me. I know better. However, I won't say anything as long as you apologize to Spencer and swear not to do any more dirty work."

"I'm not going to apologize to anyone."

"My mother is driving us to Dancing Deer after school today. So tell your dad. We'll pick you up at your house around four."

"Uh Lydia, you realize that if I own up to messing with someone's racer, I'll be disqualified."

"You should have thought of that before you sent Proctor, Alvin, and Don to do your dirty deed."

"You know their names?"

"Rex, everyone knows their names. Those boys are proud of what they've done and have discretely bragged about it to their friends. Then their friends told their friends and so on. I've heard the police in Dancing Deer are trying to get our judge to extradite the three to

Dancing Deer to stand trial. They're going to offer clemency to the first boy who gives state's evidence by providing the name of the one who put them up to it."

"Okay, I'll be ready at four."

That afternoon Sydney Rene brought Lydia and Rex to the hospital in Dancing Deer. The three walked up to the information desk. The woman seated looked at Sydney and said, "May I help you?"

Sydney pointed to Lydia, who said, "Ma'am, we've come to see Spencer Poindexter."

"He's sitting in a wheelchair waiting to go home."

Rex asked, "How bad was he hurt?"

"No broken bones. Just the normal assortment of cuts and bruises. He still has one swollen knee and is recovering from a concussion. It could have been much worse. The doctor thinks he was traveling over fifty miles per hour when he crashed." She paused a moment then asked an orderly to escort the three visitors to where Spencer was waiting.

"Hey, Spencer. I hear you had an exciting ride," said Rex.

"Yeah, I guess so."

"I'm glad we caught you before someone whisked you away. I want to introduce you to Lydia Danella and her mother, Mrs. Thompkins. Ladies this is the star soap box derby racer who tried to take a shortcut to the finish line last Saturday."

Spencer tried to stand up to shake their hands but was not able to do so and fell back into the wheelchair.

Sydney said, "Don't get up for us, Spencer. We just wanted to see how you were holding up. Is there anything you need while your body heals?"

"No, ma'am but thanks for asking."

Lydia said, "Exactly what happened anyway? Your picture made the front page of the *Skunk Hollow Fever* and I was worried you were seriously injured."

"I appreciate your concern, Lydia." Spencer turned his head. "Rex, did you come to see if I would still be in the race?"

"Not really. You're tough Spencer. It'll take more than a little spill to sideline you. No, I came because Lydia said she wanted to meet a real hero and I said I knew one."

"I'm no hero. But I think you and I now have another item in common."

"And that would be?" said Rex.

"A healthy regard for a soap box derby racer too fast for its own good."

"Amen to that, brother."

"Lydia, as to what happened, the Dancing Deer City Council did not realize they had cordoned off a track too long and too steep. I understand Wylie made it through the curves by slowing his car down before coming to each."

"And how did he do that?" asked Lydia.

"He ran off the road. The uneven terrain and the weeds in the ditch reduced his speed by twenty percent or more. So when he got back on the road at the slower speed he was able to negotiate the curves without becoming airborne."

"So him running in the ditch was done on purpose?" said Lydia.

"Yep. I voted him captain of the Dancing Deer Daredevils."

"So, you don't think someone sabotaged your car?"

"Why would anyone want to do that?"

Lydia said, "I don't know. I thought when your steering wheel came off someone must have tampered with it."

"I haven't looked at my racer yet so, I guess, that's a possibility but I was trying to slow it down by zigzagging from lane to lane and that required fast turning. I'll check it out, but really I think I was putting too much pressure on a piece of equipment not designed to be manhandled in such a way."

"And you'll be well enough in four weeks to participate in the local race in Skunk Hollow?" said Lydia.

"I'm more worried about the *Orphan Express*. The windshield is shattered, the front axle is bent, and there are cosmetic damages all over the body. I have six sponsors but their money has already been spent."

Lydia's mother said, "Let me make an announcement right now. The Peoples Bank and Trust of Skunk Hollow would like to add our name to your group of sponsors. Lydia, hand me your pen. Do you think you could add its logo for two hundred dollars?"

"Mrs. Thompkins, I'd like to do that very much but I can't. Both towns are territorial and me adding you as a sponsor would be like General Custer strapping on Geronimo's tomahawk."

"Or like Geronimo trading his war bonnet for Custer's military hat. Wait a minute; I think he did that. But I see your point, Spencer. You do what you have to and if you change your mind, you can have the money without telling anyone where it came from."

"Is your bank sponsoring *The Wind*?"

"No. *The Wind* arrived by truck already built." Said Sydney.

"Delivered? Already built?"

"Ladies, I told my dad we'd be back early," said Rex. "Also, I've got homework and, besides, I have to write letters. Oh, and I have to cook our dinner."

Lydia looked sternly at Rex. "What are you planning on cooking for dinner?"

"Come on. I'll tell you on the way."

CHAPTER 34 – LAURIE'S DETECTIVE AGENCY

Early May, 1947

The *Orphan Express* lay on the table.

Laurie thought she'd examine Spencer's racer. She wanted to report what was damaged, what had to be fixed or replaced to make it race ready, and what caused the steering wheel to come off. Where was that steering wheel? She had Spencer's helmet, his goggles, all four tires, and a mangled windshield—but no steering wheel.

Edwin sat in his wheelchair watching Laurie sort through the wreckage that was once Spencer's *piece de resistance.*

Edwin said, "What's missing?"

"The steering wheel."

"Spencer was holding it high in the air when he left the road. I bet the thing went flying when he crashed. Let's go look for it."

Later that morning Edwin, Issie, and Laurie scoured the crash site looking for the lost steering wheel. They eventually found it hiding under a pile of leaves.

Back in the workshop, Edwin had the steering wheel in his lap. With Laurie writing down every detail of what needed to be fixed to bring the *Orphan Express* back to its pristine condition, Edwin examined the steering wheel. "Laurie, look around the floorboard for a bolt."

Laurie had to climb inside with a flashlight before she could locate the bolt—or what was left of the bolt. "Edwin, I think this might be part of it." She handed Edwin a short circular length of metal covered with grooves and attached nut.

"Now if you could hand me a magnifying glass."

"Edwin, I will be so glad when you will be well enough to get things for yourself. So, so glad."

"I thought you liked doing things for me."

"Oh, Edwin, I do. And I shouldn't have said that." Laurie thought for a moment. "Maybe, I should have been born a princess with people doing things for me. But, where would be the fun in that?" Laurie was now deep in reflection. "It's like taking a road trip. Getting to the destination is the objective but sometimes the getting there is where the fun is."

"Pretty deep thinking, young lady. You might someday go around the country giving lectures, telling people how to live a happy life."

"You can make money doing that?"

"Yep. Mark Twain lost all his money backing a contraption called a Compositor. When he declared bankruptcy he vowed all his creditors would get paid. Then he started touring the country giving lectures. He made people laugh, he gave them a view of themselves from a different perspective, he made them aware that life was interesting and fun to be participating in."

"Did he pay his creditors off?"

"Yep. Had to add a tour to most of Europe and Australia to get it done though."

Edwin took his magnifying glass to look at the remnant of a broken bolt and nut. "Laurie, I think we need to go see Wylie Santos."

Wylie's mother told Edwin and Laurie that her son now lived in a shed out back. With their imagination questioning why Wylie had moved into the shed, Laurie pushed Edwin around the house on a gravel walkway. Wylie was sitting astride a short stool buffing his racer with a fluffy white mitt. "Hello, Laurie, Mr. Stanky. What are you two up to?"

Edwin said, "Wylie, we need for you to take off a bolt on the *Hillbilly Hobo* so we can compare it to one from the *Orphan Express*."

"Something wrong with yours?"

"It might have been tampered with."

"Oh, man. I knew it. I haven't let the *Hillbilly Hobo* out of my sight. No one is allowed to even touch it unless I'm there supervising. I even moved out of the house. Made a bed over there in a corner. Mom brings my meals."

"That might have been a wise move."

In a few minutes Edwin had Wylie's bolt sitting beside the broken one from Spencer's racer. He looked at them through a powerful magnifying glass then turned over Spencer's bolt. Edwin then took a small screwdriver to help count the grooves on both bolts. After several minutes of close examination, Edwin sat back in his wheelchair and said, "Yep. Someone cut the bolt with a hacksaw. They only left two threads to hold on the steering wheel. A little vibration and it came off in spencer's hand with the end of the screw and the nut falling to the floorboard."

"Holy cow. Spencer could have been killed."

"Wylie, has anybody tried to do anything to the *Hillbilly Hobo*?"

"I don't think so. It drove good the only opportunity I've had to drive it. However, now I'll be more observant than ever." Wylie sat down next to Laurie, who had climbed on a pile of lumber covered by a canvas tarp.

"Laurie, I've heard you helped line up Spencer's sponsors. Did you also do their advertisements on the *Orphan Express*?"

"Yes."

"Maybe I could hire you to help me. I've heard you turned down some potential sponsors saying you were limiting the number to six."

"Spencer told me how much money he needed and six were all we required. I might have to add another now that he has to make repairs."

"Some people have all the luck."

"Wylie, you have your share of luck and then some. How did you get in and out of the ditch without crashing?"

"The first time, I was going so fast I lost control but managed to get my nerves back and, through sheer determination, bounced back on the road. I lost some speed in the ditch so, after that, I used the ditch to reduce my speed anytime it was getting out of hand. That was one scary ride."

"So do you need more sponsors?"

"No. I just feel like I'm in this by myself and would like someone to enjoy my victory with."

"Wylie, I'm helping Spencer."

"Okay, but if he loses a heat come over to the *Hillbilly Hobo's* pit."

"Would I have to push you to the starting line?"

"Naw. I got someone to do that. All you'd have to do is wear a *Hillbilly Hobo* jersey and stand around looking pretty."

"I'll think about it, Wylie."

157

CHAPTER 35 – HOWDY
May, 1947

Howdy drove into Skunk Hollow. It was a new chapter in his life and he was looking forward to being in charge, to feeling important, and to have money in his pocket. No longer did he need to spend his summers working for pennies as a summer intern to some prestigious bank where the bosses lorded it over their employees. No longer did he have to forgo having a social life because he had to do research at the library or pull his hair out getting a paper turned in on time. It was now time to live.

The Peoples Bank and Trust of Skunk Hollow had asked him to become their new President. He spent two months dickering with them over the authority he would possess. He wanted it all and they wanted to retain a fair share over what they deemed important. But in the end a compromise had been reached that everyone could live with.

Howdy made a fast trip to Skunk Hollow at the beginning of the year. He brought a good friend from college and set him up as an assistant to prepare the way while he tidied up loose ends. While he was in town, he looked for a place to live and ended up buying the old Manfred Mansion.

It was the town eyesore. At about eight thousand feet of floor space, it was the largest monstrosity in town and everybody was glad to see him seduced by its wilted appeal. But, as always had been the case, Howdy visualized what it could look like, while others could not. He hired a construction crew from Fayetteville to renovate according to his dictates. It was now ready.

Howdy remained single. He'd fallen in love one time, but that romance had hit on hard times and he left to finish his education, leaving her with only questions and no answers. The young lady thought Howdy a charming man, a polite gentleman with manners, an interesting man, a man of character, a graceful man pleasing to the eyes. For the next few years, Howdy was the man she thought of when she closed her

159

eyes. But a man such as Howdy would never succumb to the wiles of a dreamer looking for her Prince Charming. He was too clever, too cagey, too focused. She let Howdy slip through her fingers with him not knowing the feelings he had aroused. Now he was back, the president of the town bank, single, and living in the newly remodeled Manfred Mansion. Howdy was worth a second effort.

At ten a.m. Howdy walked into his bank. The tellers, new account managers, loan officers, and Jumbo Johnny—the off-duty police officer working security—watched him come through the front door flashing a big smile. There were a lot of people saying, "Good morning, Mr. Monroe." Howdy waved, saluted, and somehow individually greeted each person he passed.

Andy Muldoon met Howdy as he entered the administrative office area. "Howdy, we are so glad you finally made it."

"Had to tie up some loose ends before throwing myself into your fiery furnace, Andrew."

"Actually, I've got everything under control. Our deposits and collateralized loans are up, delinquencies are down, and our employee turnover rate is practically zero."

"That's wonderful." Howdy turned to the Administrative receptionist. After reading her badge Howdy said, "Lois, would you call Asa Thompkins? See if we can have lunch together."

"Yes, sir."

"Tell me, Asa. How are things with you?"

"About the same."

"So, you were never able to reconcile with Beatrice?"

"Hardly. Her father wouldn't let her return my calls. You know she moved into our house. My dad had to sign it over to her dad when he couldn't repay the money he borrowed to keep the bank afloat."

"Yeah, I don't understand that. Dane had part ownership in the bank. It seems like propping the bank up would be in his best interest."

"Not after my dad had to own up to how my great-grandfather Albert swindled his grandfather Woodrow."

"Asa, are all the members in your family stinkers?"

"All but me."

"Does that include Sydney Rene?"

"Yep. She's the worst one, who's still alive."

"And you haven't made up with Isabelle?"

"No. Beatrice is the one—the only one."

"You do realize that my telling her I loved her was only to make you realize what you were about to lose?"

"At the time, Howdy, I thought you had become my worst nightmare. There was no way I could compare favorably against you. I was floored when Beatrice chose me."

"Yeah, I think she thought I swayed with the wind. Not a person who could be counted on in a storm. And, probably, a liar to boot."

"Howdy, she's never said anything bad about you to me."

"Have the two of you talked about it?"

"No. I probably should have gone to her after my father passed away, but I was too dignified. And her father still hates me. Beatrice does have time to see Sydney on occasion. She's opened a new restaurant. Beatrice's going great guns with that place. She might be selling flapjacks to the lumbering trade the way the customers line up outside her front door." Asa paused a moment while he thought about his failed romance with Beatrice. He continued with, "I couldn't make it to her Grand Opening Ribbon Cutting Ceremony and, I've heard from Sydney that my presence would not be required at any future function. The Skunk Hollow City Council is more than a little mad at me."

"Let's go there together. She wouldn't have me thrown out would she?"

"Probably not. I'm all for giving it a try."

Later that day both men stepped inside the Manfred Mansion. Wilkins met them at the door.

"Your hat and coat, Mr. Monroe? And yours, Mr. Thompkins?"

"Thank you, Wilkins. Will you ask Mrs. Jenkins to fix Asa and I something for lunch? We never could get seated at Beatrice's restaurant."

"Yes, sir."

"Wilkins, we'll be in the library."

As the two men walked down the hall, Howdy put his hand on Asa's shoulder. "Asa, you look like an abandoned puppy."

"I know. I just can't get excited about anything. Your suggesting I run for mayor has been the only positive thing I've done."

"And you still love Beatrice."

"More than anything in this world."

"Then we have to develop a strategy. Do you have any ideas?"

"Howdy, you're the idea man. I can barely get up in the mornings."

Asa looked around the dark wood-paneled room. "How do you like your home. I must say I'm impressed with the job those imported carpenters did. This place is fit for a Rockefeller or a Vanderbilt."

"I knew it would be. And I am certainly happy you were able to locate Wilkins. And now you've hired me an accomplished cook."

"Yeah, but she can't cook like Beatrice."

"Let's go to a different subject. What kind of social life can I expect in Skunk Hollow?"

"Not much. If you don't mind traveling to Dancing Deer, they have live performances at the Ritz Grand Hotel and Ballroom. Sometimes they have bands, vaudeville, comediennes, plays, magic acts and their restaurant has great food, like Sacre Bleu, but a much larger facility."

"Then, we need to get something going in Skunk Hollow. When is the next city council meeting?"

"Thursday morning at ten."

"At Beatrice's restaurant?"

"I wish. That's why the city council members are mad at me. Beatrice says she can't accommodate a large party at lunch time. I think she's trying to make a statement. Some of the members are getting a petition to oust me from office, so Beatrice will let them meet at the Sacre Bleu."

"Just another reason for you and Beatrice to make amends."

"You got that right."

CHAPTER 36 – READY, SET, GO

June, 1947

For the three weeks prior to the start of the local race in Skunk Hollow, Spencer repaired the *Orphan Express*. Toby Lynch had decided that driving a soap box derby racer was not as safe as driving his father's John Deere tractor so he sold his two axles, four wheels, and steering wheel screw to Spencer and promised to be there when Spencer won on the first weekend in June.

Spencer replaced the bent front axle on his racer with one of the two he had purchased. He also used Toby's two rear wheels to replace his two front ones, re-installed his steering wheel with the screw and nut from Toby's *Screaming Eagle*, and patched the body as best he could. He was out of luck in replacing the windshield so, when it was time to take his racer to Skunk Hollow, the *Orphan Express* was mechanically sound but cosmetically impaired.

Spencer and Gus pushed the racer up the ramps into the bed of Gus's truck. As Spencer tied his racer down he ran his hand down the sleek curve of the hood and to the *Orphan Express* said, "I moved into Edwin's workshop and had my meals delivered there so I could protect you from anyone wanting to mess with you again. It's now time, girl, to show everyone what you can do." Spencer turned to Gus and said, "Let's take her to Skunk Hollow. It's time to kick butt."

Gus parked the truck and lowered his tailgate. He thought he'd sit there so he could keep an eye on Spencer's racer and observe the people milling around getting things ready for the start of the races. It was still early Friday morning. At ten a.m. on Saturday, they would start racing three cars at a time. Fifty races were scheduled for the first heat at six-minute intervals. After breaking for an hour The second heat of seventeen races would begin. At the completion of the second heat, the number of racing participants left would total seventeen.

On Sunday afternoon, the remaining three heats would be run of six, two, and then one for a total of nine races. After the final race Sunday afternoon, the winner would be announced, trophies given out, and the streets in downtown Skunk Hollow barricaded so the town could celebrate. Everything had to be finished by seven p.m.—that's when the Sunday evening services started in the protestant churches.

Today, the Friday before, the cars had to be inspected, weighed, and re-weighed with the driver inside. The applications were checked against the car and driver. And the racers numbered and assigned a time for its first race and a lane to race in. With three cars at the starting posts, nine additional cars in three lines would be queued in their assigned order. Friday was hectic, but Saturday would be much worse.

After the winner was announced on Sunday, the town would need to let off some built up steam. Everyone looked forward to the grand celebration after Skunk Hollow's first annual All American Soap Box Derby Local Race.

"Gus, let's unload. They have a secure place to park her. People can gawk. But while the inspectors make their rounds, guards will be there to keep the spectators behind a yellow rope. I have to stay with the *Orphan Express* until she passes inspection so you might as well get some breakfast. They have canopy tents set up and the food served is free."

For the remainder of the day, Spencer took care of the pre-race logistics and appraised the competition. He also made friendships with boys his own age that would last a life-time.

Standing beside *The Wind* was Rex Muldoon. "Hey, Spence, I see you got the *Orphan Express* patched up."

"Yeah. I don't think this race will be near as scary as the hair-raising event put on by my home town. Just taking out the two sweeping curves gives me give a sigh of relief."

"Good luck, Spencer. I hope you come in second."

"I'm looking forward to going against *The Wind* and don't expect to come in second even though second should be good enough to carry the day. I understand the officials have located the trucking company that delivered *The Wind*. You'll probably be disqualified."

"You can't be serious. I built *The Wind* before we moved here."

"If you really did build *The Wind* then you did a professional job. And the derby officials will not have reason to put you in jail."

"In jail?"

"Yeah. If you signed the application saying you would abide by the rules and that you built your racer without anyone helping, but are proved to be lying then you're guilty of fraud and that's a criminal offense."

CHAPTER 37 – FIRST HEAT

June, 1947

Wylie sat beside his *Hillbilly Hobo*. He had built it long and skinny. There was barely enough room for his slender body to fit. Wylie had reasoned that since the racers did not have shock absorbers, the lighter the car, the easier it could handle imperfections in the racing surface. As it turned out the light weight also hindered the car's ability to negotiate traveling through weeds and soft dirt. That was why his car slowed down in the ditch.

Wylie was one of the first boys scheduled to race. Attached to the hood just in front of the windshield, a decal prominently displayed the racer's assigned number, twenty-seven. And the number was stitched by Wylie's mother onto the fronts of four jerseys. Wylie's mother mingled in the crowd proudly displaying hers. Wylie's father wore the second. It was his responsibility to push the *Hillbilly Hobo* forward in the queue and eventually into the starting gate. Wylie wore the third jersey and held onto the fourth in case Laurie happened to drop by.

"Good morning, Wylie."

"Good morning, Laurie. You sure look pretty."

"Thank you. Would it be all right if I sported your jersey and helped out while you race then take it off when I have to help Spencer?"

"Laurie, I'm agreeable to anything you want to do. Here, I've been holding this for you." Wylie handed the jersey to Laurie.

"I'll be right back."

Thirty minutes later the *Hillbilly Hobo* was in the starting gate, Laurie had made it to the stopping area just beyond the finish line, and Wylie waited for the announcer to yell "Go" to the racers.

When the flap fell away from the front tires, the *Hillbilly Hobo* started its descent down the track. Wylie's car was always the last one out of the gate. Being the lightest car also meant he had less weight pushing against the flap. The heavier cars seemed to lurch out when the flap dropped, but the *Hillbilly Hobo* left leisurely on a slow stroll.

Wylie held the steering wheel in a death grip. With his jaw clamped tightly shut and his eyes squinting through the goggles Wylie begged, pleaded, and willed his car to catch up. "Hillbilly, Laurie is waiting for you at the finish line. You don't want to embarrass us both by sweeping in last do you?" The *Hillbilly Hobo* didn't answer. "Well, do you?" Still no answer.

At the quarter mark. The *Hillbilly Hobo* was in third place. The lead car led the second-place car by two feet, with the *Hillbilly Hobo* ten feet farther back in last place. By the half-way mark, Wylie had started to catch up. Now all three cars jockeyed for first separated by less than three feet. At the three-quarter mark, Wylie had a slight lead. One of his competitors had developed a problem and had fallen off the pace. The second car was being pummeled by a kid's fist. The boy hit multiple blows against his car's side in an effort to get it moving faster.

"Okay, Hillbilly. That's more like it. And don't scare me like that anymore. You'll make me old before my time."

Beyond the finish line an official placed a white plank with the number twenty-seven on the tote board telling everyone Wylie Santos driving car twenty-seven, Dancing Deer's *Hillbilly Hobo*, had smoked the competition in today's third race. Two other numbers were listed alongside Wylie's number. They were the winners of the two previous races.

Spencer was slated to compete in race number thirty-two. So far everything had gone without a hitch. A few racers had developed a problem or two. Some entries even had to be pushed to the finish line. There was no other way off the track for them because of the steel cable stretched between the posts.

Spencer sat in the *Orphan Express*, second in line in the near lane. Gus stood directly behind Spencer and his car. His job was to push Spencer forward as the front cars charged out of the starting gates to the finish line.

Six minutes after race number thirty-one had left, the *Orphan Express* and two competitors were ready to do combat. An official raised his flag, checked to make sure the boys were ready. Three things then happened simultaneously. One official lowered his flag, the same official yelled "Go" at top of his lungs, and a second official let the lever, holding flaps against the front tires for all three racers, to fall to the ground. All three shot out and down the track.

The *Orphan Express* had been well designed. Spencer used a wind tunnel to determine her silhouette, he used a sliding weight to balance the racer while he was sitting inside, and he had been meticulous in mounting all four tires on two exactly parallel axles. The wheels were perfectly aligned. And his efforts paid dividends. The *Orphan Express* was in the lead at the first-quarter mark. She had widened her lead by the half and by the third-quarter mark the *Orphan Express* was in the lead by fifteen feet. She eventually won by the largest margin of victory achieved after thirty-one races. The *Orphan Express* had kicked butt, but, not yet, the butt Spencer had planned.

After crossing the finish line, Spencer lowered the brake, stopped the racer, and got out. He saw his number go up on the tote board so Gus would know he had won. Several people ran up to push the *Orphan Express* onto a flatbed trailer to be hauled back to the starting area.

"That boy must know what he's talking about. I could see from here he won the race." Gus slapped his thigh then waited on the *Orphan Express* to be delivered back to his safekeeping.

CHAPTER 38 – LURED AWAY

June, 1947

Spencer hugged May, his adopted mother; Millie, his sister; and Laurie, the girl who solved his problems so he could build the racer in the first place. He thought about hugging Wylie but decided against it and slapped Wylie on his back instead.

"I'd give you a hug too, Wylie, but you and I might have to compete against each other before this thing gets decided and I don't want to get too chummy."

"I've already beaten you once, Spence. I'll be ready anytime you are."

"Now boys, I'm kinda caught in the middle of this." Laurie grabbed each boy by his arm and led them off saying, "Let's go get something to eat."

"Laurie, let me treat you. I'm feeling on top of the world right now," said Wylie.

Laurie and Wylie got their food first and went to find a place to sit while Spencer was ordering his. A young boy walked up and said, "Are you, Spencer Poindexter?"

"Yes. That would be me."

"I was told to deliver this to you and to no one else." The boy handed over a small envelope with 'Spence' written on the top in pencil.

Spencer sat down his tray of food to open the envelope. Inside was three dollars and a note. It said:

Dearest Spencer:

I told you one day I would come back for you and Millie.

Meet me at the orphanage as soon as you can on Saturday. Please don't tell anyone about this. Use the money for a bus ticket. I checked and a bus leaves Skunk Hollow at one o'clock for Dancing Deer.

Mommy has missed you son.

Love,
Mother

Spencer never picked up his tray. He stuffed the letter in his pocket and ran out the door. In fifteen minutes, he had purchased a one-way bus ticket to Dancing Deer. Twenty minutes later he was boarding the bus.

At two in the afternoon, Gus found Laurie and Wylie. "Have either of you seen Spencer? He's scheduled to race again in thirty minutes."

Laurie and Wylie shook their heads. Laurie said, "I saw Spencer reading a note then he shot out of here. He didn't say anything to us."

"Well, we better fan out and find him. If he's not there a few minutes before race-time, he'll be disqualified. Wylie, your dad is looking for you. You're scheduled to race in an hour and a half."

Laurie said, "Gus, you go back to the starting gate and wait by the racer. Wylie and I will find him."

Wylie said, "Laurie, where do you think he ran off to? Must've been something real important in that note."

"I don't know but most of the orphans somehow migrate toward each other when we find ourselves in a large gathering of people. If I can find them, we'll have the entire area covered in no time. You go to the finish line and up the right side of the track to the starting gates. I'll cover the food tents and the left side back to the starting gates."

"If he's here we'll find him."

Laurie thought that if he was not here, an entire year of preparation will have been for naught—and there would be some unhappy sponsors.

For the next twenty minutes, Laurie and Wylie searched for Spencer. Gus was beside himself when he looked at the *Orphan Express* and saw Spencer sitting in it waiting to be pushed to the starting gate. Gus said, "Boy, you're going to give me a stroke. Where have you been?"

CHAPTER 39 – SECOND HEAT
June, 1947

Spencer shrugged his shoulders. Gus wouldn't be able to hear what he said anyway. There was too much noise coming from the fans, the announcer talking over the public address system, and the dads giving last minute instructions. When the boys were ready, they signaled. The official waited another minute then raised his flag, paused, and said "Go" while lowering his flag. The flap fell away from the front tires and the second race of the second heat was underway.

The *Orphan Express* was slow to get started. It wobbled a little left and then a little right and then settled down to a straight line in the center lane. The other two cars had a sizable lead. For the *Orphan Express,* the weight was not exactly right. The driver was lighter, the grip on the steering wheel less firm, and no encouragement coming from an excited occupant.

The fans from Dancing Deer expected the *Orphan Express* to coast to another easy victory. This race was anything but easy. At the half-way mark, the race began tightening. The *Orphan Express* had now speeded up and, instead of losing ground, it was gaining. At the three-quarter mark, the *Orphan Express* had caught up to one competitor and had the other in its sights. Twenty feet from the finish line the *Orphan Express* was in second place by six inches. When the two cars crossed the finish line, the officials ruled it a photo finish. A final determination could not be made until the other races had been completed and Makepeace Kilburn had been given time to get his film developed. No one would know until Sunday if the *Orphan Express* had vanquished another competitor.

As soon as the racers had come to a complete stop, people ran onto the track to push the racers to the waiting flatbed trailer. Others wanted to tell the two drivers what an exciting race it had been.

When the fans made it to the *Orphan Express,* there was no one sitting inside. Only Spencer's helmet and goggles were there to greet the confused fans. Several people wondered what had happened to Spencer. They were no more surprised by Spencer's behavior than three boys from Skunk Hollow: Don, Proctor, and Alvin.

An hour and a half later, Wylie was in line for his second race. Directly in front of the *Hillbilly Hobo* and one lane to Wylie's right crouched *The Wind*. Rex had driven *The Wind* to a win in his first race by a wide margin. Almost everyone had picked *The Wind* as the car most likely to be the ultimate winner. Both Wylie and Spencer agreed that if anyone beat *The Wind*, that person would be driving a significant and extremely capable racer.

The two race drivers pitted against *The Wind* in this race were angry at their bad luck of having to race *The Wind* on only their second effort. Their fears were justified because *The Wind* could have beat them traveling backwards.

The *Hillbilly Hobo* also easily won against its two adversaries.

CHAPTER 40 – TWO CALLS
June, 1947

"Rex, so far, so good on your races." said Andy Muldoon, Rex's father.

"Yeah, *The Wind* is just getting started. In fact, the only real competition we got is that orphan kid from Dancing Deer and his *Orphan Express*."

"I thought as much. Maybe we should have kept our mouths shut when we picked up that race application. I think we gave the boy that final shove he needed to redress his masculinity. We'd denigrated his racer and he felt the need make us eat our words. I wouldn't be surprised if someday we find out he cheated. If he beats *The Wind*, I think we ought to claim foul and see if the authorities can determine how he did it."

"Well, maybe, but doesn't that make us look like a couple of whiney pants?"

"Rex, it's always been the way we Muldoons play the game: all out, nothing held in reserve, win at all costs That's been our motto for generations."

"I know, Dad. But I want to win without having to resort to under-handed dealings."

"Is this a new Rex? What have you done with my boy?"

"I'm still the same guy, but I've met this girl and she recognizes everything I do that I shouldn't be doing."

"A girl? Is she the girl who sometimes calls you?"

"Yeah."

Nelda brought out the soup. It was an old family recipe made from potatoes, carrots, onions, other assorted vegetables and a little chicken broth for extra kick. The main course was bell peppers crusted in saltines and filled with hamburger meat and a white Mexican cheese then completely covered with a tomato and cheese sauce and deep-fried a golden brown

"Nelda, you are in your element in the kitchen. This tastes wonderful. Do you have anything special for dessert?"

Before Nelda could answer the telephone rang. "Would you like for me to ask them to call back?"

"No. It might be my boss. He got into town a couple of days ago."

In a minute, Nelda came in, turned to Rex, and said it was for him. "She asked for you to call her back after eating. I wrote her number on the pad beside the telephone."

In a few minutes, Rex wiped away the blackberry cobbler that had dribbled down his chin and excused himself from the table. In another minute, he was on the telephone.

"Hello, Lydia. What's going on?"

"What's going on is that you and your three hoodlum friends have sunk to an all-time low."

"Whatever they did, I'm not a part of it. I told them to cease and desist."

"You get that from your military background."

"Heard it from an uncle."

"Well, you might like to know that they sent a note to Spencer pretending to be his mother. They lured him back to Dancing Deer so he couldn't compete in his second race."

"A note from his mother?"

"Yes. When Spencer's father died Spencer's mother took Spencer and his sister to the orphanage. She left saying she needed to find a better life in California. It was in the Dancing Deer paper before Christmas two years ago."

"Lydia, I didn't live here then. There is no way I would know that."

"Maybe not but your three cohorts did and they used it in a most despicable manner to help you win a race. Rex, you are not my friend anymore."

Rex went into his bedroom. He had some things to figure out.

Later that evening, the telephone rang a second time. Rex, in a mumble, said, "This prank shows signs of escalating completely out of hand." He walked into the hall and answered on the third ring.

"Hello?"

"Rex, is your dad home? This is Uncle Sonny."

"Yes, sir. I'll take him the telephone." Carrying the telephone on a long cord to his father, Rex whispered, "It's Uncle Sonny." Rex walked and stood in the doorway.

Andy put the telephone to his ear and said, "Hey, Sonny. I haven't heard from you in a while. Is everyone all right?"

"Yeah. They were here. They asked us some questions. Wanted to know how Rex developed his skill at woodworking. We told them about the box and some bird feeders Rex put together in the backyard. Then they wanted to see the workshop. They looked a long time at his tools."

"Sonny, I don't think so."

"Sure, but that's not gonna happen. We got everything covered."

"I don't think they can do that, can they? I mean, he's already graduated."

"Yeah, but Sonny. The kid's not gonna do that. No, I understand."

"Okay, Sonny. I'll take care of it."

Andy Muldoon hung up the telephone. With a downtrodden look he said to Rex, "Uncle Sonny says you have to throw the race."

"Throw the race?"

"Yeah. Either that or disqualify yourself for some technicality."

"Dad, I can't do that. I've worked too hard. I've got a whole town expecting me to win. To win for them."

"Rex, your uncle says those three officials, who were here last month, are looking for the men who actually built the two racers named *The Wind I* and *II*. If you lose, he thinks they'll lose interest. Son, you can build another one next year."

"No, Dad. I ain't gonna do it."

"I told him you wouldn't go for it. Whatever you want to do I'll stick by you, but I don't want to lose my job either. Being successful in banking is all about perception. If a man wants a loan and looks like he doesn't need the money, the bank will try its level best to force him to take the money. If a bank appears desperate, then its depositors will be clamoring at the door in long lines to take their money out. Son, if I appear to be not quite on the up and up the bank will terminate my employment. If we don't do this right, we might have to leave town with our tails dragging and our pockets empty. See if you can come up with a solution to the problem—and let me know what it is."

"Whoa, Dad. Are you talking about us being broke—for real?"

"Maybe. Or being dis-owned by the family."

CHAPTER 41 – A DETERMINATION

June, 1947

Saturday afternoon Gus looked for Spencer. He combed through the crowd gathered in the food tents, he scanned the families loading up their racers after unsuccessfully garnering a spot in Sunday's seventeen, he canvassed both sides of the racetrack from the starting gates to the finish line, and he asked everyone he knew if they'd seen his son.

Laurie, Wylie, all of Gus's friends, and all of Spencer's fellow orphan friends—now adopted, of course—also looked. It soon became apparent Spencer had left. Gus loaded up the remainder of his family and drove home.

Spencer was sitting at the kitchen table.

That evening the note from Spencer's mother and the question of who had driven the *Orphan Express* were discussed thoroughly.

Gus made wild speculations with May agreeing, but Spencer said he wanted to keep an open mind. When the facts were uncovered, the details would make sense.

Gus said, "Okay, what facts do we have about the note?"

"For one, I don't think it was from our mother. She had never been much of a nurturing person. I think she was relieved from shouldering the responsibility of parenthood when she left. And she never told Millie or I she would come back. When Dad died, Mom fell apart. She had always solved her problems by denial. With her life in shambles, she added starting over."

"So, if it wasn't your mother who would do such a despicable thing?" said Gus.

"Probably someone who didn't want me to race. Someone who thought he had a chance of winning if I was eliminated."

"Another trick like the steering wheel bolt?"

"Yeah."

"Okay, if you didn't drive in the second heat who did?"

"Gus, you said the person looked like me. Did he drive like me?"

179

"No. He was unsure at first and fell behind. The car did a few wobbles then straightened out and finished strong. We won't know until tomorrow if he won. They're going to use a photo to make a determination."

"Anything else—anything at all?"

"He sat lower than you and when he leaned forward half of his helmet . . . I'm sorry, your helmet . . . was below the windshield. Uh, where the windshield would have been had you fixed it."

"I guess that means he was shorter than me. And since the race was so close it also means the *Orphan Express* was not performing as well as it could have. That might be because the weight was wrong. If he was shorter than me, he was probably lighter in weight as well. And someone who did not want me to lose." Spencer thought for a moment. "Could it have been a girl?"

"I guess. Whoever it was did a good job imitating you. When I asked where you had been, he shrugged his shoulders. He was already sitting in the car when I walked up and it was almost time for the race so I quickly pushed him into the starting gate."

"I'll bet he didn't say anything because he thought you might recognize his voice. Would you recognize Wylie's voice?"

"Probably."

"What happened at the finish line?"

"That is the weirdest thing. One moment he was sitting in the car, and the next, the car was empty occupied only by your hat and goggles."

"Who was the first person to get to the car after the race?"

"Laurie. And then Wylie. Pretty soon there were several people congregated around the *Orphan Express* without anybody knowing what had happened to you."

"I think it had to be Laurie or Wylie. Maybe both in on it. No one else would have the audacity or be brazen enough to try such a stunt. Or to have been crafty enough to get away with it."

"But if it was Wylie, that just means now he might eventually lose to you in one of the last three heats."

"It means that Wylie thinks the *Hillbilly Hobo* can outrun the *Orphan Express* and he wants to prove it on the track, not to win through a disqualification. And then there is his need to impress Laurie."

May got up from the table saying, "I think God sent an Angel to help you, Spencer. Michael, maybe."

Sunday morning, Gus took his family to Mass but couldn't pay attention to Father Will's homily. He had too many things running through his head. After the service, he stood by the door waiting on May. She had gotten side-tracked by some of her friends and was now informing them how God had sent an Angel to drive Spencer's racer.

"Spencer go . . . no, Millie, you go tell my lovely wife we're waiting for her in the truck. We got to go to Skunk Hollow to see if the *Orphan Express* is still in the race.

Father Will grabbed Gus by the arm, "Gus, pardon me, but what is this about the Angel, Michael, driving Spencer's racer yesterday?"

"I'm sorry, Father. Spencer . . . uh . . . ."

"Gus, I saw him. I was at the finish line yelling at the top of my voice trying to help him win."

"I know. I pushed him into the starting gate. I thought it was Spencer as well. And then, as soon as the race was over, there was no one in the car. He just vanished. Spencer said someone played a trick on him by luring him to Dancing Deer. He thought his mother had come back."

"That was a detestable trick. I can see where God would intervene in such a circumstance. Did not anyone get a closer look at the driver? I mean, I would give anything to look into the face of an Angel. Gus, did you see him?"

"Yes, but he was wearing Spencer's helmet and goggles."

"But Gus, man, you might have seen an Angel."

CHAPTER 42 – THIRD AND FOURTH HEATS

June, 1947

Gus and his family parked and then walked toward the tent where the officials had set up their official headquarters. Coming outside were a jubilant Laurie holding onto the arm of Wylie.

Laurie ran to Spencer saying, "Spencer, you pulled it off. They got a picture of you winning by a nose. The guy you beat saw the photo and left for home. He must've known he'd lost because he already had his racer loaded on a trailer and his father was waiting in the truck."

Wylie said, "Congratulations, Spence. You know the *Hillbilly Hobo* and the *Orphan Express* will eventually have to shoot it out."

"I imagine I'll be disqualified. I wasn't driving the *Orphan Express* in that race."

"That wasn't you? It looked like you." said Wylie.

Laurie said, "And you have to tell them?"

"Yep. I can't, in all good consciousness, continue after breaking the rules."

"But the picture shows you winning."

"It wasn't me."

"I understand, but no one else knows." Laurie waited a moment then said, "Spencer, you have to do what you think is right."

Three officials came out of the tent. One was holding an eight by ten glossy print. One official looked left, one looked right, and the third—the official holding the photo—walked straight to Spencer.

"Mr. Poindexter, what's this about an Angel taking your place in yesterday's second heat?"

"Sir, who told you that?"

"We got a telephone call. Several telephone calls."

"I don't know who was driving my racer, but it wasn't me."

The official looked at the picture then at Spencer. "You got a twin?"

"No."

"Why weren't you driving?"

"I was taking care of some personal business."

"Rather than racing in the second heat after winning the first by a wide margin and driving a car you spent a year building?"

"Yes, sir. It was important."

"Do you not want to race one, or both, of the posted cars you were slated to go up against in the second heat? We had that pairing listed on the bulletin board yesterday afternoon."

"I think the *Orphan Express* is the fastest car here. And I have no problem competing against anyone."

"We understand your father pushed you to the starting gate. Did he not recognize you?"

"Sir, I'm Gus, Spence's father—he's my adopted son. I thought it was him."

"Thank you, sir. We have to talk this over. We'll give you our determination shortly." After saying this, the official gave the photo to one of the other two officials then all three walked back into their tent and closed the flap.

Gus said, "Spence, I need a cup of coffee."

Wylie offered Laurie a sandwich. "Thanks, Wylie. But we don't want to eat too much. Andre, the chef from the Ritz Bistro, is in a contest himself. He and the chef of Skunk Hollow's Sacre Bleu Cafe are trying to decide who's best. Their contest benefits everyone. The food is donated by the two restaurants and there will be a jar for people to vote anonymously."

"I hope those officials make their decision soon. We're supposed to start racing at two." said Wylie.

Spencer was seated by himself, deep in thought, when Lydia brought over a sandwich and sat across from him. "Would you care to share? Usually, I don't eat an entire sandwich."

"Hello, Lydia. You have a tendency to show up at the oddest times."

"Tell me how you can make that comment."

"Okay, the first time I met you I was recovering from a wreck and you had your mother bring you to Dancing Deer to meet me. You even brought Rex to show me the person responsible for my misfortune.

Then, after another prank and someone trying to convince the officials an Angel had driven the *Orphan Express* in my place, you appear again—this time offering me half of your sandwich."

"Strange, isn't it?"

"Aren't you going to ask me where I was when I should have been racing?"

"No. I know where you were."

At that moment the three officials walked into the food tent. One official said, "We have come to a unanimous decision to let you race. Our decision was based on the rationale that if God sent an Angel to take your place it would be presumptuous of us to disqualify you for something so ordained and if it wasn't an Angel then it had to be you. I mean if it looks like a duck and quacks like a duck, it must be a duck.

"It looks like you in the picture and even your father thought it was you. So you better waddle yourself to the starting gate because you race first."

Fifteen minutes prior to the first race Rex went to one of the officials saying he would not be able to continue racing.

"What is your reason for quitting?"

"My axle is bent. I don't think it would be safe to drive and I don't have time to get another."

"When are you slated to race?"

"The sixth race."

"Okay. We got time. Get in and I'll push you to the repair pit. Let's see if the repairman can fix it in time."

In three minutes the repairman had the seat out and made the comment that it looked like someone had taken a sledgehammer to the car's front axle but there was good news because he had an extra he would soon have installed. He'd get right on it.

The official slapped Rex on his back saying, "You are a lucky man, Mr. Muldoon." He then turned to the repairman and told him to make sure Mr. Muldoon and his racer made it to the starting gate in time for his race.

Spencer sat in the *Orphan Express*. He wondered what would be his next calamity. Will Lydia be there to tell him about it? Would Laurie help him to resolve it?

The official yelled, "Go." The flag came down as did the flaps holding his front tires. And the first race of the third heat was underway.

All three racers were even at fifty feet from the gate. Spencer was in the middle lane and the racer on his left was crowding him. Spencer yelled for the boy to give him room. The racer to his right was also swerving over the edges of the stripe separating Spencer's lane from his. Spencer thought he had better get in the lead and then his two adversaries could pile up together—behind him. He hunkered down low in the cockpit. Slowly the *Orphan Express* gained ground. First it was only a few inches then, by the half-way mark, he had extended it to half the length of his car.

As for gravity, it builds on itself. So a tiny excess in speed soon added a tiny excess of the original tiny excess. It was the real-world calculus in motion.

By the three-quarter mark, he was in front by ten feet and gaining more ground as he sailed to the finish line. When the flag went down, the *Orphan Express* had won by twelve feet with the other two racers, looking like twins of different colors, tied for second place and probably hauled home in the same trailer.

In the third race, the *Hillbilly Hobo* got off to another slow start. By the half-way mark, Wylie had not gained any of the lost ground and began worrying that his luck might have run out.

"Hillbilly, Laurie is waiting for you at the finish line. If we come in second, she'll head back to the *Orphan Express*. You don't want that do you? Well, then, you better find yourself another gear—a faster gear."

At the three-quarter mark, the *Hillbilly Hobo* had made up the original lost ground and would soon be in the lead—if the track were long enough.

It was another close finish for the *Hillbilly Hobo*. Wylie and his racer won by a foot. It was communicated to Makepeace Kilburn by a nod from an official; no photo was required.

Rex ran in the sixth race. *The Wind* had never lost a race and Rex tried his best to get his car scratched, but he had made the mistake of mentioning a safety problem and instantly the repair man was brought into the picture because his responsibility was to keep the racers safe for their drivers.

Rex ran his hand down the smooth exterior of his racer. "Mr. Wind, I know you have never lost a race before but you need to lose this one for my dad."

When the racers were freed from their captivity, *The Wind* jumped to an early lead. It led the entire way increasing that distance with each yard of travel. There didn't seem to be anything Rex could do. At the finish *The Wind* won by fifteen feet. Rex and *The Wind* would be doing battle in the next race against the *Orphan Express* and a second car soundly built and expertly driven by some kid from Dardanelle.

Rex's father sat down and said, "Rex, what are you doing here? Don't you race again in an hour?"

"Dad, I've figured out what to do."

"I'm glad you have, because, there are only three races left. We're now down to six racers. There are two races in the fourth heat and the winners of those two races will go against each other for the title in the fifth heat. So, with that in mind, what are you going to do?"

"I'm not going to show. When they ask me what happened, I'll explain that I forgot or I over-slept or you made me run an errand."

"No. You keep me out of this."

"This is better anyway. I didn't feel right asking *The Wind* to throw the race and I didn't want to mention any of your skullduggery."

"My skullduggery?"

"Yeah, you don't think I'm going to take any of the blame, do you?"

"So, my boy has shown up after all."

Ten minutes later the door bell rang. Rex opened to a police officer who said, "You, Rex Muldoon?"

"Yes, sir."

"Get in the car."

"Officer, I'm not to blame. I didn't know it had been built by those engineering students."

"Not the front seat, Muldoon. Get in the back."

"Oh, right. Sorry. I'm sure this can all be worked out. You see my cousin won ten years ago and he had two cars. So when Dad said he was worried about paying for my education, his brother—that would be my Uncle Sonny—sent me the second edition of *The Wind*."

"Would you shut up."

"Aren't you going to make me an offer if I'll give you a bigger fish?'

"I don't know nothing about no book, and I don't have time for fishing. I was told to bring you in for your next race." The police officer stopped his cruiser and turned to a stunned Rex. "Knock 'em dead, kid. Go on, get out."

Lydia was standing next to Spencer. "Hey, Lydia. What's up, girl." Rex crawled into *The Wind* while one of the workers pushed him into the starting gate. Under his breath he said, "Whoa. That look would freeze lightning. What's with her anyway?"

The official asked if everyone was ready. He said this was the first race of the fourth heat. Each of the drivers signaled they were ready and the race began. At first it was neck and neck, then the *Orphan Express* forged ahead chewing up the asphalt and assumed the lead position by a foot. Then *The Wind* caught up and took the lead. The third car was in third place by ten feet. When the cars reached the half-way mark, the *Orphan Express* was back in the lead by inches over *The Wind*. Then it happened.

Sparks started flying from the left front wheel of *The Wind*. Rex's car jerked to the right and the third place car collided with it. The *Orphan Express* coasted to victory and of the three it was the only car to finish.

The repairman and two officials jumped the wire cable stretched between the posts and ran to the crash site. Both cars were still upright with two boys a little disoriented. The repairman helped one boy out of his racer then the other.

Rex, holding his head, said, "What happened?"

"Young man, you weren't giving your racer the respect it deserved so it rebelled."

"What?"

"You haven't been checking the grease in the wheel bearings and your left front froze up keeping that wheel from turning. You then lost control and crashed into the car two lanes over. And both of you lost to the *Orphan Express*. He services his car before every race.

Wylie saw the two-car collision and wondered how he would have fared if *The Wind* had broad-sided him. Suddenly Wylie understood. If he won the second and final race in the fourth heat he would race the *Orphan Express* for an all-expense-paid trip to Akron, Ohio for him, his family, and the *Hillbilly Hobo*. He wondered if Edwin would let Laurie go.

"Gentlemen, are you ready?"

Three drivers lined up to decide the final of the two racers destined to compete for the championship race. Each boy raised his hand to affirm his readiness. The official with the flag yelled "Go" and lowered his flag. A second official let fall the flaps holding the three racers back. Dancing Deer's *Hillbilly Hobo*, a car from Clarksville, and a third from Scranton descended the starting platform.

As usual the *Hillbilly Hobo* was the last one out of the gate. "You better get going Hillbilly. We don't get a second chance here. You're not gonna let Laurie down are you?"

At the first mark, the car from Clarksville was in the lead followed by the car from Scranton. The *Hillbilly Hobo* was taking its time and Wylie was beside himself trying to get his car moving at a faster clip.

"I can't believe this. You gonna let those two wannabes show you up? Where's your resin? Didn't I spend enough hours buffing your exterior? Hillbilly, your have to speed up—right now."

At the half-way mark the car from Scranton had forged ahead as the car from Clarksville had fallen back with the Hillbilly. Wylie loved on his car.

At the three-quarter mark Wylie had closed some of the gap between his car and the one from Scranton. "Come on Hillbilly, Laurie is waiting on you."

During the last hundred yards the *Hillbilly Hobo* took the lead. Wylie thought about attaching a rearview mirror for future races so he could keep up with the competition. In the stopping area several people made it to the *Hillbilly Hobo*. Laurie was the first one there.

"Wylie, you are such a good driver. But now you have to go head to head against Spencer and the *Orphan Express*."

"Uh, Laurie, could you give Hillbilly a hug?"

"Hug the car?"

"Yeah. I kinda promised him."

"Your car is a he. Everyone else's car is a she."

"I know. He's a lot more sensitive than most and I don't want him upset with me going into the last race."

"It would be my pleasure."

Laurie walked to the front of the car and wrapped both arms around the hood. She then planted a kiss on the windshield. "I did that for good measure."

Spencer said, "Maybe Wylie's car will take you to a movie sometime."

"Spencer, you are so funny."

There was an hour before the final race so most people were eating sack lunches they had brought. Families everywhere were sitting in lawn chairs or on quilts spread over patches of grass. Coolers on tailgates of trucks were filled with sodas and lidded canning jars of water.

Spencer said that everyone could snack if they wanted to but the town was having a celebration after the race on Main Street and the food was prepared by the two best restaurants in Northern Arkansas and paid for by the Skunk Hollow Chamber of Commerce. So Spencer, Laurie, Wylie, Edwin and his family, Gus and May Poindexter, and a few others wanting to be close to the important people ate cookies and cheese cut into squares and served with toothpicks.

CHAPTER 43 – THE FINAL RACE

June, 1947

Spencer and Wylie walked together to the starting gates. Neither spoke. When they reached the racers Spencer said, "Wylie, I plan on winning, but if I don't, I'm glad you will."

Wylie said, "Let's have a safe race and let the cars determine who wins."

Both boys got into their racers and got pushed to the starting gates by two very proud fathers.

Over a loudspeaker Asa said, "Ladies and gentlemen, this is our final race. We have two very fine racers and two brave young men. Please express your approval for their successful trip to our championship heat."

There was thunderous applause.

"Now let's see which one, either the *Hillbilly Hobo* or the *Orphan Express*, will represent the Skunk Hollow All American Soap Box Derby Local Race in Akron, Ohio. I now give it back to these amazing officials."

"This is the final heat. Are you gentlemen ready?"

Both contestants raised their right hands affirming they were ready. The official paused, then yelled, "Go" and lowered his flag. The second official let fall the flaps holding the two racers back. The two cars jumped out of the gate. This time the *Hillbilly Hobo* was out first and had a foot lead by the first-quarter mark.

Spencer said to his car, "I knew Wylie had built a good racer and fast, but I wasn't aware it was this fast."

At the half-way mark, the *Hillbilly Hobo* was in the lead by two feet. Wylie said, "Hillbilly, you do realize she's my girlfriend. I'm not saying she shouldn't give you a hug every once in a while, but . . . but . . . let's win this race and we can discuss it later."

At the three-quarter mark, the *Orphan Express* had closed the gap to a foot or less. To most spectators the cars were running neck and neck and it had been that way from the time they started. Makepeace was standing with his camera mounted on a tripod looking across the track and down the tape designating the finish. He held a remote activate button on a wire coming from his camera. The cars were closing and they looked like they were locked in step.

A hundred yards short of the finish line the *Orphan Express* had closed to even."

"For heaven's sake, Hillbilly, I'll let Laurie drive you herself."

When the two cars crossed the finish line Makepeace took their picture, the officials said they could not determine the winner, and the fans knew they had seen a wonderful race and hated that one would have to lose. They wouldn't find out which was the winner until the next day.

Gus and Wylie's father congratulated their sons and both went to bring over their trucks. Workers pushed the racers up ramps and tied them down. Then everybody started walking toward Main Street. Several people shook the boys' hands and told them how exciting the race had been.

CHAPTER 44 – CELEBRATION PARTY

June, 1947

Howdy shook Asa's hand. "Congratulations Asa. You make a wonderful Master of Ceremony. And this is the first time Skunk Hollow has ever bested Dancing Deer at anything."

"Yeah but Dancing Deer entered two racers and they came in first and second."

"Dancing Deer and Skunk Hollow had nothing to do with that. Those boys won on their own, and they would have excelled if they had entered from Pea Patch."

"You know, you're right. And I've not heard anyone say anything negative about the outcome or about any racer cheating or the officiating being partial. I'm as pleased as punch."

"Good. Let's join the celebration."

Skunk Hollow had put up roadblocks to cordon off one block of Main Street. Tables were set up on the road, each with a floral centerpiece. And a platform on wheels had been pulled to the middle of the tables trailing a confusion of wiring. Band members ascended the platform and soon had their instruments and microphones arranged on stands. Presently they began tuning their instruments and thumping the microphones.

Wylie and his family, Spencer and his family, and Laurie were escorted to a table directly in front of the stage. Spencer asked if additional tables could be added beside theirs for the other members of Laurie's family and the sponsors for both racers. He then placed a napkin in his chair and another in an adjacent chair before excusing himself. Spencer started walking through the throng of people. He found her sitting with her mother, the mayor, and a few other important-looking people.

Every male diner at the table stood when Spencer approached. Hands were extended, and congratulations were voiced by everyone there. Spencer addressed Sydney Rene. "Ma'am, would you allow Lydia to sit at the Winner's Table?"

"You'll have to ask her. But it's all right with me."

Spencer turned to Lydia. "Lydia would you join me at the Winner's Table? We have a seat there with your name on it."

On the walk back Spencer said, "Were you the one who drove the *Orphan Express* in the second heat?"

"Am I in trouble?"

"No."

"Well, I'm not saying. But I would have had that Angel not appeared."

Asa and Howdy stood in line with plates in hand. Beatrice stood next to Andre several feet behind the serving stations. The two chefs were involved in a spirited talk with hand gestures and an occasional whisper. At the serving stations some attendants—all women—wore blue uniforms covered with a flowery print and the words Sacre Bleu Cafe emblazoned on their bibs while others—all male—wore starched white uniforms embroidered in gold with the words Ritz Grand Hotel and Ballroom Bistro above their pockets.

It was not apparent which server was working at which station nor who had cooked the food. They were all working together in harmony and talking with each other like they were long lost friends.

Asa said to Howdy, "This is an unexpected turn of events. How do I compete with him?"

Howdy said, "Have you thought of learning to cook?"

The End

Author Bio

Ron Lambert, an Examined Life

As an accountant in a small West Texas town, I spend my days studying the bank statements and tax returns of other people's businesses. I classify, summarize, and display their financial transactions in some meaningful format. I love creating order out of chaos.

I'm middle-aged and twice married—with the second blessed from heaven. Four grown children, their children, two bobbing tails of barking energy, and one sly cat round out my cache of treasure.

Over the years, I have owned and operated two boutique retail stores, several service businesses, one ranch, and one restaurant. I have been prosperous and poor, with wild fluctuations in between. At present, being neither rich nor destitute, I consider my status as deeply entrenched in middle class—a term bandied about by politicians and economists.

In an effort to restore my youth, I purchased an old sofa on two wheels. Since that initial existential groping, I have occasionally strapped sacks of clothes, maps, and a compass that doesn't seem to work onto the back cushion. After kissing my wife, I set out for adventure and story. Usually, after only a week or so, I realize what I left behind was more important than what I set out to find and drive a day and a night hell-bent-for-leather back home.

I then settle into an old and comfortable routine. I read a few books, attend a few plays, daydream of new horizons, and plan my next adventure. I kept a journal on my first excursion. It was such an exhilarating experience: rewriting the journal and incorporating the pictures I took, that I became intoxicated to the point I wrote a novel.

At present, with pen on fire, I have just finished my eighth book— actually traveling in untested waters by writing a book for young adults. I'll win prestigious awards and be asked to speak at the local library if someone would read what I have written.

If you're looking for an evening spent with colorful and mesmerizing characters, if you want to immerse yourself in a rollicking good story, enthrall yourself to the point of madness, go two days without bathing, then have I got a story for you.

Additional Novels

The Dancing Deer Story

All books are available as Trade Paperbacks in perfect binding at www.printersguildpublishing.com and from several fine retailers in Columbus and Weimar, Texas.

Dancing Deer (Book 1)

Dancing Deer is the embodiment of small-town America. When asked, she sent her sons to war. This is the story of The Calhoun—one of those boys. It's also about his fellow combatants, the men he served, the men he fought, and the women he loved.

There is the French Resistance, the German Gestapo, Midge at the Mike, Anzio Annie, the Gustav Line, and the US Army's Forty-Fifth Infantry campaigning from Sicily through Italy, France, and Germany to push back the formidable Germans. But this story is so much more.

Find a comfortable chair and settle in with a great new book. You won't be disappointed.

The Last Dance (Book 2)

Bill Potter is charged with murdering his Friday night squeeze. His bumbling lawyer steps out of a dead-end job of contracts and leases to save Bill from being strapped to "Old Spanky." Bill's wife returns after a twenty year absence to muddy the waters and it's up to her and Pepe, the womanizing Resistance fighter and WWI spy from France, to solve the case.

The Measure of a Man (Book 3)

A group of Cuban immigrants decide to barnstorm the Midwest, entertaining the towns they come to with a game of ball. When they get to Dancing Deer the men on the city council con Bill Potter into a wager for more than they could afford to lose. Bill's position is that the Men from Dancing Deer will prevail. With a team of misfits and one win under their belts, Bill goes searching for a new manager. His ex-wife is traveling throughout the Western US with Pepe, the French womanizer. She knows more about ball than anyone and he has to convince her to come back and once again save him from the wolves at the door.

Lost in Appalachia (Book 4)

The head of Dancing Deer's Police Department is lost in the mountains of West Virginia. Suffering from an injury, he can't remember who he is or why he's lost. Two kids take him in and hide him from a determined fiancée. The chief of police is in the process of teaching the kids how to read when the fiancée posts a big reward for knowledge of his whereabouts. The chief thinks he must have committed a major crime for someone to pony up such a large bounty.

While the chief awaits the inevitable and worries about what kind of person he really is and what crimes he's committed, the children take measures into their own hands. Their rationale is there will be no one to teach them to read if their new friend is carted off to jail.

Christmas in Dancing Deer (Book 5)

St. Bartholomew's is consolidating its orphanage, but the children don't want to be separated. They come up with an alternative plan to present to the church, but the women of Dancing Deer bring the orphan girls into their homes for the holidays. The orphan boys leave on their own in the snow three days before Christmas and spend a night with a burdened bank robber in a desolated cabin.

Beggarman, Thief (Book 6)

A story of a bank robber who finds his moment of epiphany in a shack with six lost little boys. He goes home after twenty years on the lamb to have Christmas with his family and to right his wrongs. But he finds his past is in hot pursuit and the new life he has found is in jeopardy. He runs away in the clutches of a pretty lady evangelist who is taking her show on the road to the very town where he committed his last crime.

Toe to Toe with A Drunken Philosopher (Book 7)

This is really one story in three parts. First we have the high school philosophy teacher who has to resign his position much as Aristotle had to when the authorities in Athens came looking for him. Part number two is of an indigent Irish family who emigrate from the Emerald Isle. The little Irish boy in the family grows up to become a priest. The third part pits the philosopher and the priest in a contest of wits.

Racing the Wind (Book 8, Written for young adults but not yet finished)

A story of a boy with plans someday to build bridges or design skyscrapers. He decides to pay for his education by building a racer and winning the Soapbox Derby. Problems, orchestrated by his main adversary, creep into the racer's production. The boy has to rely on the help of a fellow classmate—a girl—to find the source of his problem and to finish the racer and the race.

For All the Marbles (Book 9, Written for children but just now seeping into my consciousness)

Eston's best friend, Ben, is a little older, a little bigger, and a lot slower. The other kids have always taken advantage of Ben. Now a bully has won all of Ben's marbles. Eston promised he'd win them back but ended up losing his as well. This is the story of how Eston takes a dangerous new course of action: one that will cleanse the schoolyard of bullying and win back the lost loot.

www.ingramcontent.com/pod-product-compliance
Lightning Source LLC
Chambersburg PA
CBHW050532260626
47157CB00004B/1573